FAM

JOHN SHUPECK

NIGHTMARE PRESS

Edited by Megan Nevins of Ember & Ink

Cover by Megan Nevins of Ember & Ink

ISBN: 978-1-64905-040-3

LCCN: 2020930290

DEDICATION

To Megan, for coming into my life and giving me the motivation and want to strive for not just better, but the best. You have inspired me in ways I couldn't even imagine, and you are what is making the publishing of this book possible. I love you so much.

CHAPTER 1

August 17th, 2009 is the day Dustin Taylor's brother, Trevor, died. November 24th, 2016 is the day Trevor came back.

Dustin and Trevor possessed a very dysfunctional—if not outright abusive—relationship. Trevor was six years' Dustin's senior, in life surviving to the age of seventeen to his younger brother's eleven. Trevor exposed Dustin to all sorts of debaucheries that a troubled teenager might face, the younger brother following along every step of the way, not even realizing what he was experiencing half the time.

Huffing a gallon of gasoline together in the shed behind their house; stealing their mother's Honda Civic for secret joy rides late at night, almost wrecking numerous times; Trevor convincing Dustin to skip school to drink liquor at his buddy's house while the two older boys cooked meth in the basement. These are but just a few examples of the types of inappropriate activities the child was coerced into engaging in, all to appease who he thought was the coolest person in the universe.

Trevor and Dustin's mom didn't think it was cool,

however. While never fully privy to the happenings of her sons, she was well aware of the disturbing psyche her oldest had taken on in his later years, along with the effect it was having on his sibling.

Several times, Trevor had gotten violent with her, on one occasion almost breaking her arm with one well-placed punch. She'd had to wear a sling for almost two weeks, explaining to her co-workers that she had taken a nasty spill down the stairs while taking trash out in the middle of the night.

"Damn cat got right under me, knocked me clean off my feet," she had said, more than a hint of an embarrassed blush lighting her cheeks. Her friend and coworker, Sheila, had just nodded along, holding her eyes on the pot of coffee she was brewing, not daring to meet her friend's gaze. (The story of Trevor and the ongoing domestic issues at home had well spread around town by that point.)

Slowly but surely, Dustin had begun exhibiting similar behaviors as the boys spent more and more "quality time" together. It was only a little bit at first, but soon, he was morphing into a miniature replica of Trevor and all the toxic behavior that came with him.

"Stick the stupid curfew up your ass!" he had once screamed at his mother when being stopped from leaving with Trevor on one particular evening.

"Yeah, fucking cunt. It's not like you ever cared before. You're turning him into a pussy." Trevor looked down at Dustin. "All right, I guess you're gonna be a little b-y-atch. I'm out." He slammed the door, leaving Dustin to stand there without his backup support as their mother broke into hyster-ical sobs.

Of course, Trevor had come back later that night after Mom was asleep to collect little bro, just as he had done countless other nights. And Dustin had been more than willing to go along, just as he had been countless other nights.

"You really are going to be a little bitch," Trevor had said, a forty of St. Ives in his hand as he sped down Center Street in his boy Mark's car. "I should have left you home, Mr. Mommy Man. Hit this." He handed Dustin the malt liquor, which he chugged as hard as he could until he almost gagged it up.

"Little bitch, just like I said. Fuckin' give me that." He snatched the bottle from Dustin and took a big swig, the little boy staring at the garbage-strewn floor of the car, holding back tears.

Codependency was a word that could not begin to describe what the older brother held over the other. Domination, possession, and personality annihilation were all factors that played into their relationship, traits that would have continued well into their adulthoods, had fate not intervened.

It was a balmy night in northern West Virginia when the explosion happened. Trevor had been downstairs, cooking meth with his old buddy, Mark. The two were currently indulging in something they had both sworn not to do months prior—getting high on their own supply. Dustin had been made to stay at home, a decision that would be once again flagrantly disobeyed once their mother had fallen asleep for work.

"Dude, why's your little brother gotta be here all the time?" Mark asked while holding his lighter under a brown-stained pipe. "He's a fuckin' kid. If he sees all this and narcs on us, we're going to be in deep shit." He took a big hit of the meth, careful to blow the smoke away from their equipment.

"I'm teaching him to be a fuckin' man," Trevor said, reaching for the pipe. "Somebody got to." He gave Mark a big smile, exposing yellow teeth that were already decaying from heavy drug use.

"Whatever, dude. I'm just sayin', it's fuckin' weird."

The two teens had been up for four days at that point. Their eyes were wide and bloodshot, their hair sticking up in thick, greasy strands. John, their boss, would be arriving near midnight to see their progress. John was not someone to fuck with. He was an older biker who had lots of experience in the underground world of criminality, having at least three bodies to his name, along with countless others who probably wished they were dead.

One night six months ago, John had taken the two teens down to the Allegheny River in the middle of the night. He had recruited them for his operation two weeks earlier when they came to buy dope from him. They asked if he had a way for them to make some money. He smiled at them and said that indeed he did; they just had to prove their loyalty first. Two weeks later, they did just that.

"Lie down on the ground. Put your head by the water." John was talking to Trevor.

Trevor did as he was told, confused as to what was happening. He tipped his head to the side, his ear and cheek getting covered in muddy river water.

"John, what the fuck are we doi—"

Without warning, John dropped to his knees and placed his large hands on Trevor's head and neck, shoving his face into the water. The teenager's limbs immediately began flailing wildly, his steel-toed Timberlands kicking three-inch-deep grooves into the ground beneath them. A horrible gurgling noise began to echo throughout the woods as pockets of giant bubbles erupted in the water all around Trevor's head. The boy tried desperately to push himself up with his arms, but the much larger man's strength proved too powerful, able to hold Trevor down and drown him without much effort at all.

Mark watched on in abject terror as the feet kicked less and less and the bubbles became smaller and more infrequent. Soon, Trevor's movements stopped altogether, the only noise to be heard the soothing jingles of the many chains adorning John's biker vest and jeans.

Without a word, John pulled Trevor from the water with one hand and rolled him on his back so he was facing the stars. The boy's face was bloated and bluish, his eyes closed shut.

Pinching Trevor's nose, John took a deep breath, bending down until their lips were touching. He exhaled for five seconds. Then, he tipped Trevor's head back and pumped on his chest with both hands for thirty seconds. He repeated this sequence two more times before Trevor began coughing, spitting up mouthfuls of brown river water. He lay there gasping for a few minutes before John grabbed him by the arms and pulled him to his feet, wrapping a burly arm around his waist to steady him.

"Now…you," John said breathlessly, turning to Mark. "Lie down…on the ground."

"N-n-n-no," Mark stuttered, taking a few steps back, preparing to bolt towards the woods.

"You…lay the fuck down, or they'll never…find…your body. I swear to…God."

Mark looked side to side, trying to gauge the distance between himself, John, and the trees beyond. While strong and big, John was incredibly overweight, his gut jutting out prominently through his now-soaked Harley Davidson shirt. A chase would be a no-contest.

"I'll find you," John said coolly. "I'll find out where you live, and I'll slit your throat. Your parents won't be able to bury you. Now…lay the *fuck* down."

Whimpering, Mark stepped forward inch by agonizing inch until he was just a few feet from John and Trevor, the latter of whom was still hunched over, shaking and hyperventilating.

Tears pooled in the other boy's eyes as he assumed the push-up position and put his head above the water. Just as he yelled for John to wait, the biker grabbed him and dunked his head under. There was minimal fight in Mark, and in less than a minute and a half, his body was limp.

Likewise, reviving Mark took far less effort than Trevor, possibly due to the fact that he had expired much more quickly. (Trevor had a theory that Mark had simply held his breath and played dead, a thought he never dared speak out loud due to his fear of John and what he might do to both of them if he believed he had been duped.)

John waited until both boys had themselves together enough to pay attention to what he was about to say. Then he spoke.

"You're both mine now. I brought you to death, then I breathed you back to life. If you ever do anything against me, I'll take back the life I gave to you, not a moment's hesitation. Don't either of you ever forget that."

But the boys *had* forgotten it, and forgotten badly. John was expecting three pounds of meth that final night, and they only had less than half of that: partially because they had been too busy getting high to produce more, and partially because they had smoked a good amount of product in the process of maintaining that high.

Now they were scurrying to catch up, haphazardly dumping chemicals into flasks while alternatively smoking even *more* of their supply to keep up with the frantic pace.

"John's gonna fuckin' kill us, dude!"

"I fuckin' know, dude! We're fucked!"

"Oh fuck, oh fuck, fuck-fuck-fuck-fuck!"

"Homie, calm the fuck down!"

"I *am* fuckin' calm! What the fuck are we gonna do!?"

"I DON'T KNOW, DUDE!"

They were still in the middle of their manic scramble whenever the door upstairs slammed shut. Heavy footsteps cracked against the floorboards above, causing a flurry of dust motes to rain down on the boys. They immediately went quiet.

"Trevor! Mark! Where's my shit, boys!?"

"Yo, what time is it?" Trevor whispered.

"Bro, it ain't even 10:30 yet. He's early." There was a noticeable tremor in Mark's response, his shaking now not a byproduct of drug-induced hysteria but that of pure fear.

"Boys!?" John called out again, those boot-clad footsteps getting dangerously close to the cellar stairs. *"You better have my shit or it's gonna be a bad day for the both of you mother-fuckers!"*

"What do we do?"

"I don't know, dude. We gotta tell him something."

Trevor thought for a minute, then decided he'd better call out and say something before John made his way down.

"Yo, John! Give us five minutes! In the middle of a cook right now!"

The footsteps stopped in the kitchen, just shy of the cellar. For a moment, everything was silent, save for the rapid thumps coming from the chests of the terrified teenagers. Then the footsteps resumed, heavier and quicker in their purpose.

"You little fucks better have my shit ready or I swear to fuck!" The doorknob above began to turn.

"Fuuuuck, dude." Wanting to make it look like they were working as hard as they could, Trevor grabbed a flask off of one of the Bunsen Burners and brought it over to another one with water in it. Stinking, steaming liquid swished back and forth against the glass as a shaking hand began tipping the lip of the flask against the other one.

Loud booming slammed against the decaying wood of the stairs.

"You dumb motherfuckers! You been smoking down here!? Let me find out; boy, let me fuckin' find ou—"

John's words were cut off as Trevor tipped the contents of the boiling flask into the bottom one. Instantly, a roaring blast ricocheted throughout the neighborhood. The windows of the basement blew out into the street in large shards, followed by flames. All three occupants were killed instantly, along with an elderly neighbor next door who died from a heart attack due to the shock of the explosion.

Desta, Trevor's mother, was informed of what happened about two hours later. Tears were shed, and a heart was broken. (And underneath it all, though Desta would never admit it, an overwhelming feeling of relief was had.)

Dustin Taylor went mute for nearly two weeks. He only emoted twice during the month after his brother's death: once on the night of the explosion, and once during the wake.

While saying his final goodbyes, Dustin had fought as hard as he could to lift the top of the casket, to see his hero one last time. Despite his small frame, it had taken two of his uncles and the funeral director to pry him away, but not before he managed to slip his fingers under the lid and get a peek inside.

"No…no, no, no…*no! NO!*"

Dustin had just been able to make out the charred greenish skin surrounding Trevor's exposed orbital bone before his Uncle Doug had pulled his fingers away and the casket lid slammed shut. Then Dustin went quiet again, only speaking with nods and shakes of the head for an entire week.

As the months passed, the young boy's behavior improved remarkably. He was respectful to his mother, went to school every day, and did his homework without any fuss at all. Trevor's mark on the household seemed to have passed, tragic as the circumstances surrounding his short life had been.

It was only in the dead of the night when the house was quiet and all life seemed to have stopped that a young voice could be heard, whispering: "God, let him come back. God, please, let me see Trevor again. Bring him back to life."

Somewhere, deep in the ether where stars and dreams collide, a lone entity had heard the young boy's prayers, though no sane human mind would ever dare call it God. It had heard, and, in time, it had obliged.

CHAPTER 2

"**D**ustin! Can you grab the can of sweet peas from the cupboard? My hands are full!"

"Yeah, Mom! Just give me a minute!"

Dustin Taylor, now a robust young man of seventeen, made his way from the living room into the kitchen, savoring the familiar smells of turkey and stuffing wafting throughout the house. His grandparents would be over soon, and his mother had been a nervous wreck since the night before. Grandma had been on her ever since the death of her husband seventeen years prior, believing single motherhood to be too much for someone with two (now one) offspring to bear. The death of Trevor Taylor—though Grandma Abrams had never said it outright—reinforced this belief to the maximum.

But Dustin's mother had been doing more than okay. Did she need supplemental assistance, like SNAP benefits, or to shop at secondhand stores like Goodwill on occasion? Sure, but what single mother short of a manager for a major company wouldn't? Food was always on the table, Dustin *always* had supplies and clothes for the beginning of the school year, and not a single bill had ever been behind to the point it posed any serious threat to their lifestyles. All in all, Desta Taylor was providing just fine for the two of them, and Dustin was both proud and appreciative of her.

There had been the occasional hard time, of course—not so much financially, but on an emotional level. Desta had, after all, lost her firstborn son. No amount of time and closure would take that away. Dustin didn't have many memories of him, and, while she had many bad ones, Desta would often reminisce of Trevor before adolescence, when things were still good and the dreaded Bad Thing hadn't happened yet. (Even now, the Bad Thing was a subject she avoided thinking about with all of her internal might.)

Within a day after his death, the entire town of Berthshire had known Trevor Taylor was one member of a team that had poisoned their little community with a sickness that had never been there before. While the trio was gone, their legacy remained. Pockets of strung-out addicts roamed the town's east end like zombies, alternating from seedy bars to the streets, running from things that weren't there, terrorizing any poor out-of-towner who accidentally ventured from one side of Berthshire to the other. While Trevor and friends were gone, the meth epidemic they had started remained.

"Can't find the peas, Mom! You sure they're in the cupboard?"

Desta sighed and stopped what she was doing, putting her oven mitt and spatula on the counter. While Dustin was a good son, he could be rather flighty at times. Still, she didn't know what she would do without him.

"Oh my *God*, Dustin, not that one—the one all the canned goods are stored in." She bent under him and opened the door closer to his legs, reaching around him and grabbing the peas. He unconsciously moved back a little.

"There's canned stuff up in this one, Mom. Canned ravioli, canned Spaghettios, canned soup. A whole *shitload* of cans, in fact."

Desta stood up and turned quickly, lightly smacking Dustin in the back of the head—a feat that now took her standing on her tippy-toes to accomplish.

"*Real* canned goods, smart ass. Vegetables, fruits; you know, the stuff you never eat. And watch your mouth. You're still a little boy, despite what you might think."

"Think what you want, little one," he said in his best Andre the Giant voice. "This Sunday, I take the belt from *you*, Hogan."

She blew her lips in faux-annoyance and turned back to the counter, retrieving the can opener from one of the drawers. Everything was arranged in there to a perfect sequence of her liking, and Dustin knew better than to rummage around and muck it all up. They did maintain *some* sense of respectful boundaries, despite the way they spoke to each other at times.

"Yeah, well you better clean it up before Grandma and Grandad get here. She'll have a stroke if she hears you talking like that."

Dustin smiled big.

"And Grandad'll probably thank me. Get some decent sleep at night, finally." He snickered, pulling out an open bag of M&Ms from his pocket and popping a few in his mouth.

Staring at him in wide-eyed disbelief, Desta shook her head slowly before resuming opening the can of peas and dropping them into a pot. A wet plopping noise filled the room, a sound that made Dustin feel uncomfortable, though he knew no earthly reason as to why.

"Do we *need* to have peas?" he asked as she stirred them. "Out of all the vegetables, those are like the grossest ones known to mankind."

She turned, looking Dustin up and down. His baby gut was all but gone. He wasn't skinny by any means, but for his height and age, he was slim enough. The muscle he'd developed over the past year made him appear to be deceivingly wiry—that is, until he took his shirt off. Say what you wanted, but he was definitely his father's son.

"It might do you a little good to eat more than protein and get yourself all jittered up on pre-workout stuff and coffee. You know that garbage is unhealthier than anything you eat, right?"

Dustin popped a few more M&M's in his mouth.

"Only for people of the lollipop guild," he said with a smirk, looking down at her. "For normal-sized people like me, meat and caffeine is what we thrive on. My ancestors, the Celtic Vikings, would not have survived without it."

Desta walked over to the cabinet above the sink and pulled out a jar of oregano. She shook it at him as she spoke.

"Your ancestors," she said, "were Jewish gypsies from Poland who survived off of haluski and garbage scraps. And that's just *my* side. Don't even get me started with your father's heritage and your great-grandfather, who might or might not have served in the Third Reich as a gas chamber cleaner. You think the family get-togethers are fun now, you should have *seen* Christmases back in the late 90s." She went to one of the pots and sprinkled spices into it.

"Well, inclusiveness is what makes the world go 'round, even for Nazis." He went to dip his finger into the whipped cream of the pumpkin pie on the kitchen table.

"*HEY!*" Desta was smacking his hand before he even realized she'd turned around. "You think what your ancestors did was bad, wait till you see what I do to you if you try to touch one of my pies again!"

"How do you *do* that?" he said in complete awe. "It's like some kind of weird mom super power, or an advanced honing chip aliens implanted into your brain or something."

"You better get the hell out of here before something gets implanted into *you*. Now, go. Leave me be. Let me have some semblance of peace before I get berated for raising a six-foot-four animal all evening. Not that such criticisms are wrong."

"Grrrr," he said, then reached out and pinched her leg. She jumped and giggled at the same time, beating him on the arm with the spatula she was holding.

"GET OUT! NOW!" She was still giggling.

"Yes, my height-deprived mistress. I shall do as you ask." He pinched her one last time, eliciting another onslaught of the giggles as she turned and pushed him to the doorway.

He left her to continue cooking, venturing back to the living room. With a sigh, he fell on the couch and stretched his feet out, reaching for the X-Box controller on the coffee table. Just as he grabbed it, Dustin spotted something odd. On the glass surface was a big ring of moisture right next to the remote control. Had he had a drink there earlier? No, and even if he had, he would have used a coaster, as Mom had trained him to do.

(LITTLE B-Y-ATCH!)

Besides, that ring was too big to be from one of the glasses they had or a pop can. It was almost like it had come from a bottle of some sort, like wine, or a two-liter, or…or a forty, like

(St. Ives)

Really weird. Whatever it was, Mom would flip out if she walked in and saw it there. While he loved her to death, Dustin could barely tolerate her neurotic tendencies at times. Sometimes, she could be a real

(FUCKIN' CUNT!)

nag. He still cared for her deeply, though, despite her somewhat OCD-like tendencies.

Quickly, he grabbed a rag from one of the compartments underneath the coffee table and wiped the phantom ring away. Then, as carefully as he could, he folded the rag in just the way his mother liked and put it back. It wouldn't be a huge deal if he didn't do it perfectly, but she was already in hyper-manic mode, and Dustin had no desire to hear her complain any more than she already was.

Feeling content with his cleaning job, Dustin leaned back

again and grabbed the controller. He pressed the big silver circle in the middle until all the buttons came alight. Moments later, a familiar noise blared across the sound bar beneath the TV as the large X-Box logo faded into view. Time to shoot some bad guys up on Call of Duty before the grandparents arrived.

He scrolled through until he found the correct game and pressed the little blue X button. A loading screen of animated soldiers in camo fatigues showed for a few seconds, then the main screen opened up. New Game, Multiplayer, Prague. Another loading screen, and then Dustin was in the game.

His soldier avatar came into view, fully in military gear, AR-15 in hand. The timer counted down, and then it was off to the races. Dustin ran through war-torn streets and buildings, unloading magazine after magazine into countless enemies, moving at the right time when he was fired upon, shooting back when they were reloading and unprepared for it. He got caught occasionally by frags and opposing gunfire, but all in all, he was playing one of the best games he ever had.

"YEAH, YEAH, HOW'S THAT FEEL, YOU LITTLE DICK GREMLIN!?" Dustin screamed into his Turtle Beach headset. *"AWWWW, YOU CRYING!? LITTLE HOE!"*

"Dustiiiiin!" Desta called out. "Your grandparents are going to be at the door any minute. If they hear you saying this shit, the X-Box is going into a wood chipper!"

"Fuck," he muttered under his breath, reaching up and switching the microphone off. It was one thing to be screaming and talking shit whenever he was losing; it was at a whole other level when he could do so while mercilessly dominating everyone. The tears and rage quitting from full-grown adults who were double his age was worth the effort alone.

So focused was he, Dustin did not notice the chat above the game or how people kept tagging him with laughing emojis. A notification popped up from his buddy Steve, saying he had sent a private message, but Dustin decided to read it later. He was on a kill streak of a lifetime and stopping to see Steve calling him a fag or one of his other childish insults was of no interest to him at that moment. Dustin was in the Zone, and nothing was taking him out of it.

Finally, the game ended. Eagerly, he waited for the stat screen to pop up. A few moments, and there it was: 39 kills, 2 deaths, 13 assists. This blew his old record out of the water.

Feeling elated, Dustin went to start a new game when there was a knock at the front door. He moved his eyes to the analog clock above the TV. 4:30.

"Fuuuuck," he said under his breath while exiting the game. Grandma and Grandad were here. The fun was done for the day.

"Shut that damn thing off," Mom whispered to him as she sped walked past the living room to the foyer. He was just about to do as she asked when he remembered Steve's message from a few minutes ago. He quickly went to it as Desta greeted her parents at the front door.

Dude, what is up with ur screen name? Some1 hack ur account?

Confused, Dustin flicked over to his account settings. He hadn't changed his username in months: DustyRoads187, named after his favorite wrestler from the 80s. Was this Steve messing with him? If so, he was going to get a swift shot in the nuts the next time Dustin saw him.

He scrolled through the options on the X-Box's top menu until the information screen came on. Dustin read over it quickly, needing to do a double-take. His hand flew to his mouth, stifling a gasp. It couldn't be; it was impossible. Nobody else knew that but him.

"Mom, you didn't have to bring potato salad! I made a ton of it already!" Desta was yelling from the foyer. Dustin barely heard. The world around him was an abstract array of colors and noises in which he was oblivious to.

"Dustin! Get up and come say hello to Grandma and Grandad!"

"O-okay!" he called back, standing up on wobbly legs. He set the X-Box to shut down with the controller. Just before the screen went black, he saw it again, and this time he had to hold back a scream.

Name: Dustin Taylor

Username: MrMommyMan1998

"Dustin! Get up and help carry some of this stuff!"

"Y-y-yeah, okay."

He looked down at the controller and rubbed his fingers along the plastic. Unnoticeable at first, but there was a gritty residue along the edges. He lifted it up to his eyes to examine more closely.

"I'M NOT SAYING IT AGAIN!"

"Okay, I'm coming!"

He set the controller down and went out to greet his grandparents and carry in the unnecessary amount of food they'd brought. When he went to hug his grandfather, he cringed back a little bit. In his last days, his older brother, Trevor, had developed unnatural wrinkles and lines around his mouth and eyes—a consequence of the amount of meth and various other street drugs he'd been consuming. Looking at Grandad was like looking at Trevor, had he survived for another few decades. The one who had called him the name that was now in full display for the entire world to see. Mr. Mommy Man.

"Hey, buddy! How've ya been?"

He forced himself to accept his grandfather's hug. With the uncanny resemblance and frailty of the older man's frame, Dustin could not help but feel as if he was embracing a corpse.

CHAPTER 3

Dinner went as it usually did. Grandma prattled on about all the ladies at bingo and what gossips they were; Mom ignored Grandma and went on and on about Dustin's scholastic accomplishments; Grandad ignored them both and sucked down Guinnesses like they were water while watching the Steelers game on his phone.

Dustin was quiet as usual, though not for his usual reasons. If anyone was paying attention, they would have noticed how his plate went almost entirely uneaten, or how he kept glancing towards a certain room in the hallway, as if he was expecting someone to come *(shambling)* walking out at any second. A special guest, one who hadn't joined them for Thanksgiving in quite some time. He'd be hungry, considering all the years he'd been away, down...there, in the grave.

"Dustin, you've barely eaten a thing."

He snapped his head up.

"Wha-huh? Oh, yeah, sorry. Great potato salad, Grandma."

He scooped up a big spoonful and forced it down. "Great" was a little bit of an overstatement; it was okay, once you got past all the broken eggshells.

"Well, thank you, Dusty," Grandma said proudly. "This time, I used organic chicken eggs rather than store-bought. So many chemicals and preservatives they use. It's why you look thirty-two instead of seventeen."

"They're great," Dustin mumbled out through a mouthful of, at best, mediocre potato salad, made with *organic* eggs.

"You can never go wrong with natural. When I was your age, that's all we had, even in the stores."

No, when he was my age, Dustin thought. When he was my age, he was on top of the world. Banging the girls, huffing the gas, letting his little bro try beer and coke. When he was my age, he had the skin blown off his body, his teeth out of his skull. I remember…I remember…seeing it…in the casket.

"Yeah, Grandma, it's all pretty gross now," was all Dustin could manage to say. Grandma nodded; Grandad grunted; Mom was looking at him funny. He cast his eyes down to his plate. He'd gotten over this in therapy years ago. Why was he obsessing about Trevor again like this?

They all finished eating and made their way to the living room, save for Dustin, who hadn't eaten much at all. He hung out for around a half an hour, then dipped for his bedroom. He actually didn't mind chilling with the old heads; he didn't want to be alone. But sitting in there, looking at the coffee table where that condensation ring had been…at the X-Box. He just couldn't.

As he walked down the hallway, he slowed down a little when going past one room—the one that had been a storage area for the past four years. Mom had been hesitant in changing it at first. Despite all the terror he had introduced into her life, Trevor had still been Desta's son, and his room was left intact for the first couple of years after he died as a sort of twisted, delinquent memorial to him.

Dustin almost never went in that room. No reason in particular; there was just simply nothing in there that gave him purpose to enter. Besides Mom's insane organizational system that would get him murdered if it were put into even the slightest bit of disarray, what lay buried in that room were a lot of painful memories that Dustin would rather leave forgotten. While the essence of Trevor was gone, the objects that comprised his expression of self were still in there, buried in some box. Just like him.

No, there was no reason to go in that room at all. But still, Dustin found himself stopping at that plain white door, saw himself reaching for the knob as if he was somewhere else, looking through the window of someone else's perspective, unable to control what they were doing. Opening the door slowly, body shaking, terrified of what he might find inside…

"HEY!"

"MOTHERFUCK! HOLY SHIT!"

Desta Taylor stomped her way back through the hallway. The slap she applied to the back of her son's head was not so gentle this time around.

"OW! Mom!"

Desta whisper-yelled, "What the *hell* is wrong with you!? Your grandparents might have heard that!"

"Desta? Is everything okay?" While Grandma had mastered the art of *sounding* concerned, there was a clear undertone of what she claimed to dislike about her chirpy bingo friends: snooping.

"Everything's fine, Mom! Dustin stepped on a thumbtack!"

"Okay, dear! Your father was really concerned!"

Rolling her eyes, Desta turned back to Dustin. First, she looked to the half-opened storage room, then back to him, an eyebrow raised.

"What were you doing in there?" she said in that same aggressive whisper. "There's nothing in there for you."

"Uh, well, well, you see, I, uh…" Dustin scanned his mind quickly, finally settling on what he thought sounded like a cogent excuse. "Box fan! For my room! The AC's been acting funny, and it's really hot back there."

"Oh, shit!" Desta exclaimed in her normal voice. "I just bought that thing six months ago! Why didn't you tell me while the warranty was still good?" She was already making her way over to his room.

"Uh, Mom, I mean, it's no big deal!" Dustin was trailing closely behind her, trying to think of something to stop her from going in, but too little, too late. Desta had entered his bedroom before he even had the last sentence out.

By the time he caught up to her, Dustin's mom was already fiddling with the AC unit in the window, pressing different buttons, trying various settings. He could immediately feel cold air blowing on his face and arms.

"Now, *what's* the problem?" Desta said distractedly, still checking settings on the LCD screen.

"It...it wouldn't turn on?" was all he could think of saying.

She turned to him, her eyebrows now furrowed in annoyance.

"It wouldn't *turn on*? The thing behind me that was already running before I walked in the room?"

"Ye-yeah. That's, that's right. I hit the On button earlier, and nothing happened. No lights, no air. Nothin'."

"Uhh-huh," Desta replied, putting her hands on her hips. That was never a good sign. "And you were going to take this perfectly working fifty-pound unit behind me out of the window so you could put in...a *box fan?*"

"It wasn't working before," he said in a small voice, looking at the carpet.

"Dustin," Desta said in a stern voice while approaching him slowly, hands still on her hips.

"Yes?"

"I love you, but you can be really stupid sometimes. Wash up, then come out and apologize for your mouth. Grandma will never let me hear the end of it if you don't." With that, she walked right past him and closed the door behind her.

Dustin stared at the AC unit in disgust, as if it doing what it was supposed to be doing had maliciously spited him in some way. It responded by continuing to assault him with a gust of sickeningly comfortable cold air. The red lights on the LCD screen stared at him mockingly, like Hal 5000 from *2001: A Space Odyssey*.

"Stupid fucking thing," he muttered. "Always working when I don't want you to."

He exhaled a big breath, then turned to do as his mother requested and wash up. He went to the bathroom beside his room and cleaned his hands and face with soap and water. Then he was out and walking down the hall. In the stress of everything, he had completely forgotten the reason for the lie about the AC unit until he was approaching the door to the right—Trevor's door.

NO, the storage room door! Dustin chided himself internally.

He went to peek inside when he noticed something odd: the door was closed again. Had he unconsciously pulled it shut when following Mom to his room? Had *she* possibly closed it on her way back to the living room? Surely it had to be one of these two things. Grandma and Grandad hadn't been back here, and the windows were closed, so a breeze couldn't have done it. Him or Mom—probably Mom. That was the answer. Nothing strange going on here.

(MrMommyMan1998)

Before he realized it, Dustin was in the kitchen, trying to catch his breath. For the first time since childhood, he had run down the hallway, scared of an unseen monster.

CHAPTER 4

Dustin helped Desta clean up and pack away Thanksgiving dinner after his grandparents left. Hanging out with them had brought about some sense of normalcy, giving him time to think as someone nearing adulthood and not as a small child, scared of the boogieman in his closet.

The ring on the coffee table had been from a bowl of ramen he had eaten earlier in the afternoon. He could have sworn he'd put a coaster under it, but it definitely wouldn't be the first time he meant to do such a thing and forgot.

The very specific screen name on the X-Box? Steve had his password to use Game Pass. In all their years of knowing each other, Dustin must have told Steve the embarrassing nickname Trevor had given him, probably while smoking a blunt behind the gym at a basketball game or something. Weed always made him blurt stuff out and then forget it. (He'd already made a plan to give Steve a nice ball tap in the gym before home room next week.)

The closing of Trev—the *storage room*—door was such a minute issue that he didn't even bother asking his mom if she had done it. She probably wouldn't even remember if she had, and he damn sure couldn't remember if he did, so it made the entire subject kind of moot. It wasn't even that much of a mystery, to be honest.

It was later in the night now. Dustin was lying on his bed, scrolling through YouTube videos on his phone. The last thing he watched was by his favorite influencer of all time, L.A. Beast. In this particular instance, Beast had consumed an entire box of sidewalk chalk, then proceeded to chuck it up violently into a bucket, no censorship added.

Despite such intellectually stimulating material taking up his attention, Dustin was still distracted. Not by anything in particular; the fears he'd harbored earlier felt so silly now. Thinking about it, what *had* he actually been scared of? That his crazy drug addict brother had magically reappeared in the house to terrorize him again? Even if such a thing were remotely possible, the sheer physics of the universe would never allow it. Bodies decay, skin deteriorates, the leftovers get eaten by insects. How can a skeleton walk with no muscle, breathe with no lungs, see with no eyes? The eyes had probably gone first.

That's your fucking brother you're thinking about, dude! The voice inside of him now was not the usual quiet, serene one he heard. It was offended, disgusted. This was no way to be thinking, regardless of what Trevor had done to him.

Dustin had done family therapy for the first few years after Trevor's passing. Many things had transpired that he was not even aware of in regards to the severity of the trauma he endured. It wasn't until much later when he sat down and said these things out loud to an adult that he realized, and even then it had taken years to understand the true impact Trevor's actions had had on him.

Dustin was exposed to things between the ages of nine and eleven that a lot of people never experienced in their entire lifetimes, whether it was drugs, illegal activities such as car theft, drinking copious amounts of alcohol before even being out of elementary school, etc. There were a lot of things he had done as a child that he would never *dare* think of doing now.

Did he smoke the occasional joint sometimes, maybe sneak a few shots in at family barbecues? What teenager his age didn't? A little dabbling in theft with some candy bars when he was thirteen? Sure, why not? Almost every kid did it at some point.

But what Trevor had him do—no, *forced* him to do—when he was so young, that was nothing short of both tragic and damaging.

Mom knew a bit, but not about the really, really bad stuff, and she probably never would. Even Dustin himself had blocked a lot of it out as the years went by, making a subconscious decision soon after Trevor's death to erase a lot of the uglier stuff, choosing to remember what he was like before the Bad Thing happened (whatever the Bad Thing was; beyond fleeting glimpses in his dreams, he had blocked that out, too). He had very few memories from that time, but he held onto and cherished the ones he did for all they were worth.

He swiped down on his phone, scrolling through more videos. It was getting late now, and he'd have to go to bed soon. Well, he didn't *have* to, but Mom really didn't like for him to sleep in late, and she was off from work tomorrow. She'd be pounding on his door in the morning before long, and if there was anything he hated more than waking up early, it was being forcefully woken up by the hammering of Desta's iron fist.

Dustin reached over and switched his Steelers lamp off, stretching and yawning as he did so. Immediately, he was enshrouded in darkness, save for the little square of light emanating from his iPhone. He settled for an old L.A. Beast video he had already watched and put the volume on low, just so there would be a little light and sound to help him go to sleep. He yawned one last time, rolled over, and closed his eyes, counting cats jumping over a little white fence until slumber took him.

<---------->

Knock, Knock, Knock
Dustin's eyes rolled beneath their lids, but he did not stir.
Knock, Knock-Knock, Knock-Knock-Knock, Knock
More insistent now.
"Mmm," Dustin moaned, rolling over on his pillow.
KNOCK, KNOCK, KNOCK!
"Okay, Mom, I'm up. Just give me five minutes, okay?"
Silence
Moaning more, Dustin ran his tongue along his sleep-dry lips, not opening his eyes. For five minutes he lay there like that, hoping to catch just a few more Z's, but no luck. Mom's iron fist had ruled the day again.

"Fucking bullshit," he mumbled as he pushed himself up. "Off school for the week and still can't sleep in. Let me go to *her* room at 5:00 AM on an off day and see…"

His thought trailed off. With his eyes open now, he immediately sensed that something was wrong. Everything was where it was supposed to be; nothing seemed to be amiss. The AC was running fine—a fact that he was now happy about. In fact, the whole room was pretty chilly. So, what in the world had him feeling so off?

It was when he picked up the phone from beside his pillows that he realized. The same L.A. Beast video was playing on near-silent mode. Dustin looked down below the man puking a canned chicken into a toilet to see the time-stamp. 45.4 minutes.

Next, his eyes jumped to the top right corner of the screen. The confusion grew into puzzlement.

2:17 AM.

Dustin looked up now, finally realizing what had caused his initial disquiet. It was still pitch dark outside his window, late enough to not even be considered morning yet. What in the worl—

Knock, Knock, Knock

Very softly now.

"Mom?" Dustin asked without thinking. He stood up slowly. The plush carpet felt soothing on his bare feet. "Mom, everything okay? You know it's, like, two in the morning, right?"

He approached and then opened the door. What greeted him was an empty hallway, the only sign of life being the white nightlight plugged into the outlet near the bathroom.

Had he been dreaming when he heard the knocking? No, because it had just happened again less than a minute ago when he was sitting up in bed, wide awake. Something was definitely off.

"Mom?" he called out, stepping onto the bare hardwood of the hall. A shiver ran up his spine from the coldness against his feet. As quietly as he could, Dustin padded his way down to the first door on the left. It was slightly open, just as it always was. He pushed forward a little and looked in.

Desta lay under her comforter, exhaling light snores. The moon peeked in through her window, illuminating her face underneath its soft glow. Some buried part of his psyche told him this was wrong; he shouldn't be in here looking at her in such a prone state.

Shaking the thought away, Dustin gripped the knob and pulled the door back to its original position, leaving it slightly ajar. He began going back to his room, walking on the balls of his heels so he didn't wake Desta (not that *she* ever made such provisions for *him* while he was sleeping). He was almost at his door when he stopped dead in his tracks. Something was off again, but this time it only took him a few seconds to realize what.

Underneath the door across from his, a thin pool of light shone out through the slit in the bottom. The storage room. *Trevor's* room. Had that been on when he first came out? It had to have been.

It's okay, Dustin. Mom was in there earlier, putting Thanksgiving stuff away. Her problem; let her take care of it tomorrow. That cool, logical voice was back now. Dustin liked this voice, despite the slight wobble that was growing ever-present in his knees.

"Yeah, she'll probably blame me for it," he whispered out loud, uncaring if he sounded crazy. Any voice, even his own, provided the illusion that there was someone else there in this dark hallway with him, with a doorway that shouldn't be lit and impossible knocks that shouldn't have been heard.

Dustin stared at the light for a very long time. It was stagnant, no shadows to break its glow, no creepy flickering like in a horror movie. The very fact that it did nothing at all was even more disconcerting. It was as if the light was sitting there watching him through the crack in the door, biding its time, waiting patiently for his curiosity to get the better of him to come and check it out.

"No," Dustin said in a voice that was somehow both his current one and another that was much younger. "I'm going back to bed. This is retarded."

With that, he turned and made his way back to his own room, heedless of how loud his footsteps might be now. He did not turn around until the door was closed and the lock in the center of the knob was engaged.

Immediately, Dustin flicked the main light on. After that, he made his way over near the bed and turned the Steelers lamp on. When that was done, he turned his phone to the newest L.A. Beast video and pushed the volume to the maximum. Finally, Dustin lay down on the bed, staring at the swirls of the paint in the ceiling until daylight broke.

The knocking never came again that night, nor were there any other odd occurrences. Only when 7:00 AM rolled around was there any activity.

<------------------------------>

He was awakened by Desta. She was sitting on his bed, shaking him angrily.

"Mom? Mom! Yo! What is your problem?"

Desta looked down at him with wide eyes.

"You scared the living shit out of me is the problem! Were you trying to give me a heart attack?"

"A heart attack? What?" He was genuinely perplexed. He'd been sleeping since daybreak.

She stood up quickly, the bed springs squeaking with the shifting of her weight. Her hands immediately found their way to her hips.

"Okay, smart ass. You got me good yesterday, but the jig is up. 'Mom, I'm going in there to get a box fan!' I can't *believe* I fell for that. I know you're stupid, but you're not *that* stupid. And locking your door now? Did you forget I have a key?"

"Mom, I don't know what you're talking abou—"

She threw her hand in front of his face.

"Don't want to hear it. You get your *ass* in there and clean it up. And everything better be put back *exactly* as I had it."

He was left there, slack-jawed and dumbfounded as Desta stomped out of the room, not even bothering to close the door behind her. He heard her booming footsteps echo through the house all the way to the living room, followed by the slamming of the front door. Listening closely, he could hear the ignition of the old Civic putter into life. And then it was gone. He was alone.

Quickly, Dustin got on his feet and ran into the hallway. What greeted him was a sight that would have mortified him just a few short hours ago: the wide-open door of the storage room.

Steeling himself and not quite as frightened in the daytime, Dustin swallowed a lump in his throat and crossed the hallway. There was no need to turn the light on, as the sun was shining through the dusty windows in all its ever-consuming glory. Dustin's jaw dropped at what he saw.

All of the totes and boxes had been moved around until they formed a circle in the center of the room. In the middle of this was their old kitchen table that had been placed in storage two years prior. It was upright, the tablecloth they had used the day before placed neatly upon it. Little animated turkeys wearing pilgrim hats and holding forks and spoons stared at him, their mouths wide open and tongues hanging out, looking as if they were ready to dine on an as-of-yet-to-be-revealed feast.

Between the two windowsills hung a banner which read HAPPY THANKSGIVING. The orange and red letters hung individually on one long string—Mom's newest decoration that she'd just taken down from the living room the night before.

Dustin walked forward as if in a fever dream, unable to comprehend what it was he was actually seeing. As he did, his bare feet came over something gravelly. He wiggled his toes. Little brown particles fell from in between them to the floor.

Bending over, he inspected closer. It was difficult to see at first because it blended in with the color of the hardwood, but close up, what he had stepped in was as clear as day.

Dirt. Course, brown, gritty dirt. It trailed all the way around the room to the far window on the right, where it abruptly stopped. Dustin followed the path. He stopped at the window and looked at the latch on top. Unlocked.

Holding in a groan, he forced himself to look down at the sill itself. Dark, greasy smudges were smeared against the white paint, ten in all, all of which trailed to the edge of the window and then outside. It was as if someone had crawled up the side of the house and let themselves in.

Someone covered in dirt. Lots and lots of dirt.

CHAPTER 5

The cleanup had been easy enough. Rearranging everything back to its original position had not been.

Desta Taylor had all of her keepsakes arranged a certain way: Dustin's things, ages 0 until now; Trevor's belongings, the same way; New Years, large to small; St. Patrick's Day, Easter, Thanksgiving, Christmas, etc. Photos had totes of their own—the older ones had boxes that had to be separated from the totes but kept close by them. Half of his morning was spent playing Tetris with knick-knacks and mementos. Every time Dustin thought he was done, he'd discover a stack he'd forgotten that had no room to be slid in with the rest. By the time he finished, he had a throbbing migraine.

Desta had returned sometime around ten. Dustin made sure to clean the dirt on the floor and windowsill before she did. He did this for two reasons: one, he knew that would make her flip out more than having her precious organizational system sabotaged; two, because it would cause her to ask questions for things that he did not know or want to know the answers to.

As he worked, what happened had become clearer and clearer to him. Someone, probably a junkie vagrant, had used a ladder to break into the house last night. Where had they gotten a ladder? Who knows what neighbor had left their garage open or forgot one outside after a long day of lawn work.

Why their house? That is where Dustin had deduced it was probably a junkie—a meth junkie, to be specific. He remembered seeing such erratic behavior from Trevor. He'd be driving down one road, think someone was following him, then suddenly switch to another road, only to switch back to the original road and repeat the process again. In a way that made no sense at all, it made perfect sense.

As for the bizarre Thanksgiving tableau...that one was a bit harder to figure out, but soon enough the answer was obvious. In their strung-out mind, the junkie hobo had realized it was the holiday and started missing their family. They went through everything and set up their own Thanksgiving. Then, when they realized they had no food, they got frustrated and left, returning the ladder they had stolen. Easy and logical enough, at least when looking at it through the eyes of a drug addict.

The scariest thing of all was the knocking. This person had actually ventured through the house, had tried to make contact with one of its occupants. Mom had left her door open, for God's sake. What if they had decided to go into her room and...

Dustin shut the thought down immediately, the possibilities of what could have happened being too much to bear. The important thing was that the worst *hadn't* happened and everyone was safe. He just needed to make sure the windows were securely locked this time, and there would be nothing else to worry about.

He finally emerged around 12:30 PM. He'd done a good

enough job getting everything put back into place. Mom would go in there and find *something* wrong—she always did —but at least he'd gotten things to a manageable level where she wouldn't have a Level 10 meltdown. She was making lunch when he walked into the kitchen.

"What, you don't want to sit at your own little table that you set for yourself?" She was at the stove with her back to him.

"No. I realized while cleaning up that it wasn't such a very funny joke, after all." He'd decided earlier not to tell her what had actually happened. No reason to freak her out even more. He thought of the knocks again now and second-guessed that decision. They had been in real danger last night.

"Oh, it was funny, plenty funny. Especially the part where I saw the light on at six o'clock in the morning and thought someone had broken in the house. You're lucky I didn't ring your neck then." Desta peeled off the top from a can of Spam and dropped the meat into a pot. A loud sizzling noise filled the kitchen.

"Yeah," Dustin said somberly. "I didn't think of that. I am really sorry."

Now Desta turned to him, her expression softened.

"You seriously need to cool it with the joking and the pranks. Yeah, it's funny sometimes, but I'm still your moth-er." She turned back to the stove. "Why don't you find your-self a girlfriend or something? At least go out sometimes instead of always being cooped up here with me...I'm sure I'm not the best company."

He pulled out a chair from under the table and took a seat.

"Because then I wouldn't be here to drive you insane, and who else would do that? You're the only woman I need in my life."

Desta blushed.

"Yeah, well that insanity is what might drive you to an early grave."

They both went silent, an unspeakable tension hanging in the air. Desta continued making lunch while Dustin scrolled through Facebook on his phone, the events of the night and morning still weighing on him heavily. As he saw the updates and ramblings of friends who weren't *really* his friends, he decided he should tell his mother about the night before. It would be unsafe and irresponsible not to. He waited until she set lunch out to bring it up. Spam and corn Mexican surprise. The perfect meal to bring up such perfect subject matter over.

"Uh, Mom," he said while squirting ketchup onto his plate.

"Yeah?" She was scrolling through the Walmart website looking for some new school shoes for him.

"About what happened last night, in the storage room."

Her eyes flicked up from the phone screen.

"Dustin, you said you were sorry and cleaned it up. As far as I'm concerned, the discussion is closed." Desta went back to scrolling.

"No, um…there's something else I have to tell you. It's really, really important."

Desta switched off her phone and set it on the table.

"Okay, what is it?"

"Eh-hem." He cleared his throat. "What happened, with the table and decorations and everything being moved around…that wasn't me. I didn't do that."

"What…what are you talking about, Dustin?" She was eyeing him up and down as if he were a bug in a display case.

"The whole thing last night, I didn't do that. Someone knocked on my door around two in the morning, and I thought it was you. I went down to your room to check, but you were still sleeping. I came back, and the light was on in the storage room. I saw it under the door." He breathed deeply, having said all of that in one breath.

For a while, it was quiet. Desta regarded her own thumbs while Dustin kept his gaze stuck on the bowl of Mexican surprise, which wasn't really much of a surprise at all. What he had just laid on her, now *that* was a surprise—the mother of all surprises, in fact.

"So," Desta said through gritted teeth, "you're telling me that someone—a stranger—was in the house last night, and your reaction with your mother, two doors down in an unlocked room, was to lock yourself away? While someone was roaming around and doing *God* knows what? That's how you responded, and you're only just *now* telling me about this?"

Dustin said in that man-child's voice, "I didn't know anyone broke in until I saw the room today. I thought you left the light on yesterday."

Stirring her food with a fork, Desta stared towards the back door for a few moments. Her silence was always worse than her yelling. The calm was here now; the storm would soon pour down. The question was, would it be quick and over with, or would it be a deluge?

"Mom? Mom, please say something. I'm so sorry. I didn't even think of what happened until like two hours ago. I was just as shocked as you."

"Did you check the rest of the house?"

"Huh? What? Mom, I don't know what you me—"

Desta slammed her hand on the table.

"Someone broke in last night, Dustin. They had access to everything. Did you check the rest of the house to make sure nothing was missing or that they aren't still here?" Desta spoke these last words slowly and over-pronounced, as if she were speaking to the village idiot.

Immediately, all the color drained from Dustin's face. He jumped to his feet and slammed his chair in.

"Shit! Mom, I'm so sorry! I'll check right now!" He rushed back into the hallway as Desta sat with her head in her hands, indicating a very bad headache was coming, possibly a migraine.

The house wasn't very big, being a one-story ranch with a basement. Dustin had all the rooms and closets cleared within five minutes. He'd found more of that course dirt trailing from the storage room to his room, confirming that he had indeed had a visitor the night before. He checked further down to see if the same person had gone near Desta's room, but the floor was squeaky clean, just as she had left it after sweeping and mopping the day before. The upstairs was safe.

Dustin returned to his mother and reported his findings, explaining how it seemed like their visitor had gone to his room and nowhere else. He did find minor traces of dirt going the opposite way towards the kitchen, but he assumed he had tracked that himself while going up and down the hallway.

"And what about the basement?"

"Huh?"

Desta breathed deeply, collecting herself.

"If they would hide anywhere else, it would be in the basement. All the storage stuff is up here, and we only have the washer and dryer down there, not that you ever use them. They could still be down there."

Dustin's heart leapt in his chest; his stomach was doing flip-flops on itself. He had thought of the basement, but there was no dirt trail leading to that door—only in the storage room, to his door, and a tiny bit going the other way. With that much dirt, it would have been apparent if their visitor had veered towards the kitchen, where the basement door was. (He remembered the traces he found going in that direction and tried to push the thought from his mind.)

"No one went down there, Mom. Trust me. It was only in Trevor's room, and that was it."

"What did you just say?"

Dustin thought for a second and corrected himself.

"The storage room. Sorry."

"We need to have that basement checked. I'm calling the police." Desta picked her phone up and began dialing.

"Mom!" Dustin protested. "It's just some homeless junkie. And besides, he's probably long gone from here. He probably messed with stuff in the room, passed out, woke up, and left. I can check down there. It's not a problem."

The phone was still in Desta's hand, though he hadn't heard a voice answer on the other end yet. Why had he made such a stupid offer to do something like that? He was a decent size, as well as strong; he'd taken up weightlifting at school the semester before last. A little 120-pound tweaker wouldn't stand a chance against him, assuming that's who the new occupant of the house had been. Judging by the little one-person party set up in the storage room last night, this was almost certainly the case.

But druggies possessed more than just natural strength. In the case of meth heads, they could be straight up crazy. Dustin had witnessed this firsthand, more times than he would have liked to admit. While having the body of a full-grown man, he had never been in a fist fight his entire life, let alone with someone blown out of their minds on whatever the hell it was they were on. Did they have a weapon, something that could cut him down at the knees, perhaps literally?

One time, he'd been hanging out in town with Steve. It was at night after a basketball game, and they had just gotten slushies from the 7-11 near the east end of town. He knew to steer clear of there, but Steve had offered to walk a couple of girls from class home who lived in the area. Unfortunately, as with most young men his age, little brain had trumped big brain and he'd gone along.

They were turning the corner from the 7-11 to Center Street when a man suddenly jumped out at them from an alley.

"Are you with them!?" He was wearing an old Simpsons shirt with holes all through it and stained jean shorts that hadn't been washed in the better part of a week. In his hand, he held a three-foot-long machete.

"Uh, n-n-no, man, we aren't with anybody. Just trying to walk home, that's all." It's a good thing Steve had been there. Dustin did not handle confrontations well at all, let alone one as sudden and serious as this one.

"I SAID, ARE YOU WITH THEM!?" Dustin could vividly remember the junkie's spittle hitting him on the side of the face when he screamed. Then, the junkie had held up the machete and pointed the blade at Steve. They were both only fifteen at the time.

"No," Steve had said as Dustin practically cowered behind him. "We aren't with anybody." So much confidence, so many guts. Dustin remembered wishing how much he could have been like Steve in that moment.

The junkie regarded them, scanning Steve up and down. Then, inexplicably, he lowered the machete back to his side. He'd had no teeth despite having been no more than thirty years old—Dustin remembered that part clearly.

"You guys are cool," the junkie said, calm now. "Hey, either of you have ten bucks I can borrow?"

"No, man, sorry. We spent it all on the slurpees we got." Steve damn well had ten dollars on him; Dustin had seen it when he opened his wallet in the store. What a fuckin' *boss.*

"Okay," said the junkie. "Just don't fuckin' tell *them,* okay? They're looking for me."

"Will do. Have a good night, buddy." And with that, Steve waved Dustin to come with him. He did, giving a wide berth between himself and the alley that the junkie had slunk back into. Fuckin' *boss.*

Dustin wished Steve were here with him now as he turned without waiting for Desta's reply. He made his way to the basement door beside the refrigerator. He looked at the floor before going down. Was that dirt, perhaps even an outline of a footprint? No, too dark. Just spilled coffee grounds that hadn't made it to the trash.

You're being paranoid, Taylor. Just be like Steve. Steve wouldn't be scared. Steve would knock that scuzzy bum right the fuck out.

Yeah, but Steve was also an asshole who had changed his X-Box screen name and made everyone laugh at him. Steve could suck a fat one as far as Dustin was concerned. (But was that *really* Steve who had done that?)

Dustin turned the knob and opened the door. He heard Desta's heavy breathing behind him and put it out of his mind. He had a job to protect her after how much she'd protected him throughout his life, and he planned on following through with it.

"Don't close the door. Okay?" Desta sounded uncharacteristically scared, like a little girl.

"I won't, promise." He hadn't planned to. While he was feeling a particular type of bravado at that moment, he wasn't feeling particularly stupid. Mom had 911 already typed into her phone, and he very much wanted her to use it if necessary.

He stepped onto the top of the stairs and flicked the switch to his right. Immediately, the large room below was awash with the bright glow of fluorescent lights. Step by step, slowly, carefully. This was a newer house, which meant there wasn't much creaking. This was good. If someone were down here, they might not be alerted to Dustin's location, giving him the element of surprise to have the advantage.

To do what, Rambo? Sing them to death with a song from show choir? Who the fuck are you fooling?

Dustin was now nearing the bottom of the stairs. The brand new Maytag washer and dryer combo stared back at him, their insides dark and unmoving. Mom had just bought that a few weeks ago and had been particularly proud of it. They hadn't had a brand new washer and dryer since…ever. The previous set it replaced had been old, carried over from the former tenants. A big square of dirt on the floor beside the Maytag marked where the older dryer had sat. They must not have filled that part in with concrete during renovations; Dustin had never noticed it before.

Cautiously, he left the final step and moved forward. First, he looked in the cranny to the left where all their board games were stacked. Once that was given the all clear, he came around the stairs to the cranny on the right, which was currently empty. Nothing.

"You big pussy," he said to himself quietly. "All that for nothing. Just a good for nothing junkie that left. Grow up, Dustin."

Dustin made his way up the stairs. He turned the lights off and shut the door, satisfied he could tell Mom that everything was okay. This was good, at least for now. The party was just getting started; no need to hasten things any quicker than they needed to be.

"Nope, nothing down there, Mom. Everything is allllll clear."

"You sure you checked everywhere? Where we keep the games?"

"Yes, Mother. And the cubbyhole on the other side. Nothing down there but detergent and the odors of dirty socks past."

"Good. Now, I want you to go through and make sure all the windows are locked and latched."

"I shall do that, my small friend. Would you like a peanut, little lady?"

"Yeah, a peanut to shove right up your ass. Now come on. Windows."

"Ooookaaay."

The muffled voices faded away as their owners' footsteps fell from the kitchen and went further back into the house.

She never locked the windows before. Many adventures would have been aborted if she had. But Desta Taylor was nothing if not a creature of habit. Even so many years later, that could be counted on. Otherwise, the adventures yesterday wouldn't have been a possibility. But good ol' Desta had come through, just as she always had. Some things never changed.

While Dustin's bravery was commendable, it was not a trait that allowed him to be very scrupulous. If he had been, he would have realized there was a three-foot gap between the wall and Desta's brand-new, super-duper, ultra-deluxe washer, just big enough to hide a body standing behind it. Maybe not a body like Dustin's; he was *such* a big boy now! Mom must have been feeding him well. The meals were never that good back in the day, that's for sure.

But a much skinnier, much more *flexible* body? The Maytag had done just fine with that. Seventeen is such a fine age, but boy, does it make you so *stupid*. He should know— seventeen had just about killed him.

Just about.

The voices behind the door were back now. They were laughing, full of mirth and warmth. He had never heard them sound that way. He tried to laugh too, but all that came out were croaking barks as clods of dirt fell from his mouth to the floor. That was okay; he was never one for jokes, anyway. But he did like to have fun. It was his only joy in life, and man, oh man, was he *itching* to have some fun again.

But not now. Now was Dark Time. He'd had a lot of that recently—in fact, he could barely remember a time without it. The dark was so cold and desolate, nothing to be had but shivering whimpers and thoughts of times before everything went black. Before the Void. Before the madness.

It stayed standing exactly as it was for hours, limbs outstretched like a spider splayed against its web. Dark Time would be ending soon, and then, the night.

CHAPTER 6

"**D**ude, you were completely camping! What? No, you were camping! That hit...yo, that hit was complete fucking *bullshit!* Okay, okay, bitch, we'll see what happens when I respawn. I...*YO, FUCKING PUSSY!*"

"Dustin Taylor! You watch your fucking mouth right now, or I'm disconnecting the wi-fi! Keep testing me."

"Sorry, Mom!"

Such talk was expected around this time of the night for Desta, who just wanted to lie in bed and read her romance novel in peace. Why Dustin felt the need to wait until ten o'clock in the evening to log onto the X-Box and obscenely banter with his friends for a game that did not in the least bit simulate real military combat, she would never know.

Dustin's father had been a *real* soldier—a Marine, in fact. She had met him at the restaurant she waitressed at in town twenty-four years ago and was instantly smitten. He'd grown back most of his hair and had traded his fatigues for a dress shirt and a tie by that point, but the muscles he'd built during his time in the service were still very much in play.

He'd come there every morning, ordering the same thing:

four egg whites, three strips of extra crispy bacon, and two slices of lightly buttered toast, always on rye. Occasionally, he'd have a cheat day and get a short stack of heavily syruped pancakes, but this was rare. Norm Taylor was still on active duty and could have been called back at any time, and he wanted to be ready if he was.

Had Norm lived, both Trevor and Dustin would have had a much different upbringing. While not a harsh man by any sense of the word, he was disciplined, a quality he expected from those around him, especially his family. Wake up at least an hour before school, homework between 1700 and 1900, bath time and story by 2100, in bed by 2200, no room for negotiation. A steady schedule and routine were very important to him, and it was a system that Desta thrived under.

The effects of his untimely death while serving in Iraq had been devastating, not just to Desta, but to their entire family structure. Trevor eventually stopped going to bed at a regular hour. Soon, he stopped doing his homework, paying attention in school, or listening to what she told him to do. By the time he was thirteen, Trevor was a distant imitation of the sweet child he'd been just a few years before. He had gotten caught drinking multiple times already, and Desta suspected he had been smoking for at least a year.

By age fourteen, he had graduated to smoking weed and stealing pills out of her purse. At fifteen, he'd done his first stint at juvenile hall. Sixteen, he was completely gone, not beyond all repair, but to the point it would have taken a literal miracle for it to be reversed. And all the while, he blamed her, saying *she* had led him down this path, that *she* had been the one to destroy his life and make him feel forced to do the things he was doing. All Desta had done was love him and try to protect him. Was that such a bad thing for a mother to do?

If Norm had lived, if the Bad Thing hadn't happened when Trevor was twelve, there's no telling how things may have turned out. An uncontrollable chain of events had transpired, one thing after the other that led to Trevor's downward spiral, and then, ultimate demise. Things had been so, so bad. He'd almost been taken from her, and then he'd almost taken Dustin away from her, and there wasn't a single thing she could have done to stop any of it.

"Motherfucking asshole! Go suck down a dick sandwich, fucking cock monkey!"

Desta smiled in spite of herself. Despite everything that had happened, things were okay. Not perfect, but okay. In a strange way, Trevor's death had brought them closer together than they ever would have been. They'd depended on each other, clung to one another in those times when everything was a confusing whirlwind and emotions were scattered every which way. Dustin had needed her when Trevor was alive, and she failed him. It was not a mistake she would ever make again.

"Your mom is a hoe, fucking dick bag ass rider!"

"DUSTIN!"

"Sorry, Mom!"

She was still smiling. She had failed one of her boys, but found tenfold redemption in the other. Was he perfect? Of course not. But he was a tender soul, he cared for others, and, most importantly, he loved her. That was the only thing that was important for Desta.

She lay there like that for a while, thinking of these things well after her son's tirade ended and the house was quiet. She eventually fell asleep, the romance novel splayed open on her stomach. The moon hadn't quite reached her window yet, but it would, in time. Then, she'd be able to be seen in all of her exquisite beauty, just like last night. The thing watching from her closet waited eagerly for that time.

CHAPTER 7

The night passed without event. Dustin slept in until ol' Iron Fist had woken him up at 8:30 AM. They had an outing planned for that day: a trip to Desta's old stomping grounds up near Pittsburgh. She had a friend there that she hadn't seen in years, at least since before Trevor had become a teenager.

Desta told Dustin he didn't need to come, but after the events on Thanksgiving night, he still wasn't exactly comfortable being in the house alone. The invader was long gone by that point, but just the idea that there had been some unknown entity prowling about, having access to them at their most vulnerable moments…that unsettled him greatly.

It had taken everything within Dustin to not lock himself up before going to bed the night before. It would have been a futile effort, anyway; the wood making up the door was practically paper-thin. If someone had wanted to get through it, they would have gotten through it. But just the idea of a barrier, some resistant boundary that could provide a level of security comforted him, even if that level of security was incredibly low.

The main reason for leaving himself vulnerable was Mom.

He'd stayed awake late into the night with the volume on his phone low, listening for any potential disturbances. While not a fighter by nature, Dustin was a big guy, seemingly hitting a new growth spurt every nine months or so. He at least stood a chance of defending himself. Desta did not.

When 4:00 AM went by without any issue, he finally decided it was safe to sleep. Even then, it had taken him the better part of an hour before he did. He would lie on one side, then switch to the other, even though he normally slept on his back. He was doing everything he could to avoid that, as such a position would give him a direct line of sight to the door. Looking in that direction conjured mental imagery of some faceless fiend on the other side, dressed in all black, a glass pipe in one hand and a rusty machete in the other. He did his best to avoid thinking about such things.

Hence, he had taken Desta up on the trip to Pennsylvania. Cindy, Desta's friend, owned land that held a three-story house, a barn, and a cornfield that spanned as far as the eye could see. It was just past harvest time, and the field was still thick with stalks branching out from the ground. Just in Halloween, Cindy and her husband had cut out a haunted maze for the neighborhood children to walk through, though that had since been overgrown.

But the *real* attraction, what Cindy had here that Dustin loved more than anything: horses. Specifically, riding horses. He'd been more than overjoyed when Cindy was giving them a tour and asked if he liked to ride. He said he did, then shyly mumbled out that he didn't have riding boots with him. Cindy asked what size he wore. 10's? Cindy's husband wore 11's. They were a little loose on Dustin, but once the horse was saddled up and he sat atop it, everything felt just right.

For about two hours, he rode around the property while the two women caught up, drinking tea in the gazebo near the front of the house—a large white Victorian set in the back end of the land. They hadn't seen each other since Trevor's funeral, though they had always kept in touch.

Desta was amazed at how gracefully Cindy had aged. Besides the slightest hint of crow's feet around her eyes and a tinge of gray in her black hair, Cindy looked basically the same as she had twenty years ago. (She may have even weighed a little less, as impossible as that seemed.)

Cindy commented on how well Desta looked herself, a compliment she shrugged off with the wave of a hand and a laugh. Desta believed she had aged remarkably fast within the past ten years. She knew was still a looker for her age, but she didn't think she was anything close to what she had been in her prime, creating underlying feelings of insecurity and loneliness.

"I'm serious, Des. You look just like you did when we were teenagers. I thought you'd been Photoshopping your Facebook photos or something."

"A teenager? Ha! I looked like I was in my forties fifteen years ago. I'm lucky I still have all my hair at this point, especially living with *that* one over there." She tipped her head to Dustin off in the distance. "I'm already guaranteed to have lifelong heart problems."

Cindy picked up her leather cigarette case from the table. She popped it open and tipped it towards Desta, offering her a Misty menthol. She declined. Cindy shrugged and tapped one out for herself. She put the filter end in her mouth and lit it with the Zippo from her purse.

"Babe, if *that* kid is the worst of your problems, sign the adoption papers right now. Jeff and I would love to have him here. Put that big body to work. Plus, he'd keep the horses from getting restless." She blew out a cloud of heavy gray smoke.

"Yeah," Desta said. "Wait till he's up until midnight playing Call of Arms or whatever it is, calling his friends 'motherless cocksuckers from Satan's asshole.' You won't think he's so cute or lovable then."

Cindy waved the comment away.

"At least he's calling them motherless. Imagine what those boys on the other end are saying about *you*."

Desta considered this for a moment, then pointed to Cindy's cigarette case.

"On second thought, you mind if I grab one of those?"

Cindy pushed the case towards her. Once Desta had a cigarette out, Cindy held up the lighter to her mouth and lit it for her. The first drag sent her into a coughing fit. She hadn't smoked for at least twelve years. She looked off in the distance, making sure Dustin couldn't see her. Still on the horse, pointed in the other direction. Good.

"You really do have a good boy," Cindy said. "It is amazing, with how bad things were and how well he's turned out after all of that. It's a blessing."

Cindy did not use the word *blessing* lightly. She and her husband were hardcore Southern Baptists who applied Christian Scripture to anything and everything. The word "luck" was not in their vocabulary, replaced with phrases like God's Providence and Divine Intervention. To call something a blessing meant she believed He had placed something in someone's life for a very direct and specific purpose.

Desta let out an exaggerated sigh. "I suppose you're right. I guess I'll let him live a little longer, at least until he stops amusing or serving me. I wonder what the cap is for late-stage abortion in West Virginia."

Cindy quickly turned her head, blowing a mouthful of tea onto the concrete and grass beside her. Given her faith, no one else would be able to make such a joke and walk away without at least a verbal tongue-lashing. Except Desta. She just had a charming, matter-of-fact aura about her that Cindy couldn't get upset at. It had been that way ever since they'd met.

"Desta!"

"Just saying." Desta smiled at her while taking another hit. It was scary how quickly she could re-acclimate back into an old habit.

"So," Cindy said, looking around conspiratorially. "Any new Mr. Someone's you've been talking to?"

"I..." Desta started. "I...no. There was someone six months ago. We texted a little bit, but nothing came of it. We still say hello sometimes, but it's not going anywhere."

"I see," Cindy said while stubbing her smoke out in the ashtray on the table. "And have you been going to church? Lots of nice, single men in there. Treat you good."

There it was. Every single time they spoke. Cindy would bring up church at least once. While Desta knew her friend had good intentions, the preaching spiel got old really fast. It was easy to Bible thump when you had an executive husband, a castle, and no worries in the world. Common folk like her couldn't afford to put hope in the unknown when the known had already proven to be so dismal. Losing a child changes you, especially when they had already been lost before they died. She had Dustin, and that's all she really needed.

"No. I haven't had time after I became manager of the diner. I work from pretty much daybreak to closing on Sundays. Short-staffed." Would that be enough to satisfy Cindy and drop the church talk, at least for now?

"Most places have Bible studies during the week. Plus, there's online stuff now."

"I'll go, promise."

Cindy nodded. It seemed like she didn't quite have the fight in her today to argue. Good. After all the craziness the other night, Desta just wanted a place she could go to relax with minimal stress. She and Dustin, together. She was really happy he had come with her.

"So..." Cindy continued. "He getting his license yet?" She

pointed a thumb at Dustin. He was at the stalls now, dismounting the horse she had named Black Velvet.

Desta nodded.

"Still on his permit. I made him wait a year because he can be a little...reckless. But no, he's doing good. He's learning much faster than Trev—" She cut herself off.

"Yeah, I remember you having a difficult time with him. That's good that Dustin's taking to it quickly, though." Cindy pulled out another smoke and lit it while Desta was just finishing hers. Cindy didn't like chain smoking, but the current subject matter necessitated it.

"*Everything* is easier with Dustin. I know he's messed around, probably dabbled in some weed. But overall, he is a really good kid, ain't he?"

Cindy nodded, watching the boy take his boots off.

"It gets better, Des. You've seen that. Trevor was a good kid, too. He went through a lot—things that were out of your control. You have to believe that, babe." Despite her words, Cindy felt a knot in her stomach just from saying Trevor's name.

Choking back a sob, Desta nodded, affirming that to herself just as much as Cindy. Her friend reached out, taking Desta's hand in hers.

"I know," Desta said, voice heavy with unshed tears. "Despite everything, I miss him. Who he *was*. I wish he could get another chance."

Cindy used her free hand to wipe Desta's eyes.

"He's still here, sweetie. All the time. Watching you and Dustin, seeing how well you both are doing. And you know what? He's happy, too. You have to believe that."

Looking at her friend, Desta nodded again, but this time it was a lie. Where Trevor was was not a happy place; it never had been. And if he could see them, see how well Dustin in particular was doing right at that moment...there was no secondhand joy. Just anger, pain, and resentment, just as there always had been.

CHAPTER 8

The horse stable was a few hundred yards away from the house. Dustin could see the two women in the gazebo, but from his vantage point, they looked like little colorful dots. Was that Mom *smoking*? He couldn't tell from this far away, but he thought she was. Aunt Cindy was a smoker. She'd had one in her hand when he first got out of the car and hugged her (a gesture he didn't mind at all; Aunt Cindy was looking good for her age, though the gross smoke smell was a bit of a turn-off). Hopefully, Mom wasn't picking the habit back up.

He walked into the stable and set Uncle Jeff's boots down in front of Black Velvet's stall. As he did, the horse approached him shyly, sticking its nose through an opening between the slats. Dustin caressed it tenderly.

"Good boy," he cooed. "Good boy. Not so scared of me now, yeah? We went on an adventure today. You want a carrot?"

He went over to the black sack hanging on the stable door and pulled a long orange carrot from one of the pouches. The three other horses snorted in excitement, all approaching their respective openings.

"Nope, not for you guys. This is for Velvet. I'll feed you all later."

Dustin wiped at his eyes with the back of his hand. He'd taken a Claritin last night in anticipation of today's visit, but his hay fever was still poking through a little bit. It was such a shame, seeing as how much he loved the outdoors and animals. The smells weren't always the greatest, but freshly cut grass and bales of hay were the number one thing that could always put his mind at ease. In another life—perhaps one with more money—he could see himself being a farmer, mowing through acres of land on a big tractor in the mornings, picking corn in the afternoons, tending to the animals before sunset. All things he would kill to do every day if only they had the means to do so. (And if he could work ten damn minutes without going into a sneezing fit.)

Dustin approached Black Velvet's stall, holding the carrot out.

"Here you go, boy. Easy now. Easy...easy."

The horse regarded him with its wide brown eyes, then gently bit down on the skinny end of the carrot, allowing Dustin to feed it until there wasn't enough left for him to hold. He watched as it gobbled up the rest in loud chomps, never taking its eyes off of him. So beautiful. He didn't want to ever leave.

Dustin stayed in the stable for a little while longer, feeding and petting the other horses, checking out the rest of the barn, enjoying the smell of the hay (what little he could smell through his half-clogged nose, that is). He lingered for as long as he could, then decided to explore the rest of the property. He was certain there were a lot of interesting things he would come across.

The farm itself was quite expansive, spanning around fifty-two acres in all. Dustin decided that instead of roaming aimlessly, he would check out the second most interesting section of the property, aside from the barn and the house: the cornfield. It was about a fifteen-minute hike from where he was at now. He looked down the hill. Mom and Aunt Cindy were still in the gazebo. He had time.

The walk to the cornfield was mostly uneventful, consisting of open land covered in a mixture of both dead and dry grass. He did come across a few interesting finds: a rusted hubcap from a really old car, some orange traffic pylons buried under a pile of mulch, a John Deere tractor from the 70s that probably hadn't run for the better part of twenty years. It was amazing how such things that cost tens of thousands of dollars just a short time ago could be so easily disregarded, left under the sun to rot. It made him a little sad to think about.

As he walked through the grass, he suddenly felt very paranoid. A few times, he stopped and looked around from all sides, swearing he heard footsteps off in the distance. There was no one around. He supposed the recent events at the house had put him a little on edge, though he saw no reason to feel that way out here. They were almost one hundred miles from Berthshire, and he highly doubted their visitor from the other night had the means or a reason to follow them. Still, he couldn't get rid of this creeping suspicion that he was being followed.

To distract himself from the paranoia, Dustin thought about other things. He'd messaged Steve the day before, letting him know how incredibly unfunny his prank with the X-Box username had been. Of course, Steve had sworn up and down it wasn't him, claiming he didn't even have access to do such a thing. If that were true, then the only other person who had the opportunity to do it was Mom, and he *knew* that possibility was off the table. The only other rational explanation he could muster up was that maybe he had done it somehow, like sleep typing or something like that, but that also made absolutely no sense. Another alternative scenario was one of the *irrational* sort, one that would make sense with the timing of things but also opened a Pandora's Box of horror that he couldn't allow himself to even consider. The break-in...the visitor, the one who set up their own private Thanksgiving in a very specific room of the house—the room that used to be occupied by the one person in the world who knew the name inputted into the X-Box. But that couldn't have happened. He saw the casket buried himself, had seen a part of the body just a few short hours before it was lowered into the ground and covered in tons of dirt. There was no way it was possible, unless, maybe...

Dustin was suddenly feeling incredibly hot. Sweat beaded on his forehead as daylight began to wane. It was almost the beginning of December. Why was it so *warm* out? It might make sense if they had gone south, like to Virginia, but they had gone northeast. It felt like it was the middle of July. He kept walking, ignoring the sounds around him and focusing on getting to his destination. He was safe out here, nothing to worry about.

Finally, Dustin reached the cornfield. Close up, he saw the tall stalks were intermittently tied to sunflower plants. Inquisitive, he walked up and inspected this anomaly, pulling on one of the stalks. Immediately, he saw the purpose of the sunflowers as the weight of the corn tried to push the plant over. Anchors, used to keep the stalks standing upright. Interesting. *Cool.*

Oh, you really think it's cool, Mr. Mommy Man? Corn really is the bee's knees, huh? You gonna go home, play your little X-Box, eat Hamburger Helper while you scroll Facebook on your phone? That's cool. I've been in the grave this whole time. Not much to play with, but there's a lot down here to play with me. The bugs, and the worms, and the maggots. Mom protects you? She never protected me. Remember what happened, little bro? Remember it. The Bad Thing...

That second voice—that hoarse, grating, raspy voice that he heard in his head sometimes. It had been so long since it had spoken to him in real life that he'd forgotten who it even belonged to. But after recent events, he now knew who it was. It was as clear as the sunny day he was standing in right now. Trevor.

"It's only in your head, Dustin," he said. "Only in your head. Trevor's dead, and he's not coming back. Never coming back, never coming back..."

His stomach knifed in on itself as he felt a hand clench itself around his shoulder blade.

"Only half right, bro." The voice was barely a voice at all, sounding more like a comical imitation of the human vocal registry, one that had been washed in a bath of acid, broken glass, and rusty razor clippings.

And yet, despite the over-the-top distortion, Dustin recognized the voice's owner immediately. Unconsciously, he cried a little as his bladder loosed itself.

"Dustin's been gone a really long time." Desta had her hand above her eyes as she searched off into the distance."

"Relax," said Cindy. "He's probably off checking out the cornfield or something. Jeff's maze might still be there."

"Yeah, maybe," Desta said, still scanning the field. "I just hope he comes back soon. It's gonna be dark, and I don't wanna hit any deer on the drive back."

"I'm sure he's fine, Des. There's no one out here except us. You need to stop being such a worrywart. It doesn't suit your complexion, my love." Now it was Cindy who shivered, remembering what happened the last time Desta's children had ventured into the cornfield alone.

Desta chuckled.

"Yeah, you're right. I'm sure the big dumb ass is fine. I just worry, y'know?"

Cindy patted Desta's hand from across the table.

"I know, sweetie. But trust me when I tell you Dustin's fine. Nothing to worry about."

"Yeah, yeah, I'm sure he is."

Dustin was on his knees at the entrance of the cornfield, that bony hand still gripping his shoulder tightly. Everything was bright orange now as the sun was beginning to set. The world looked like a mixture of being on fire and covered in blood. His damp pants and underwear clung to his thighs, his breathing was gasping wheezes. Despite his terror, he began to turn his head to see who had a hold on him.

"Don't look at me!" the thing behind him croaked. Dustin immediately pointed his head forward again.

"Good, little bro. Good, good. This is all a dream-dream-dream. You fell asleep. Riding horses. So much fun. You know Mom used to take *me* horse riding back when I was a kid? You know that, little bro-bro?"

Dustin shrieked as it shoved its fingers into the opening of his shoulder blade. "Mmm...mmm!" is all he could manage to say.

"Yeah, riding all the horses. Right here-here-here, on Aunt Cindy's ranch. You try to fuck her?"

Dustin shook his head emphatically.

"No? I guess a little faggot like you wouldn't. Fag-fag-fag-fag." It sounded like an old audiotape stuck in a loop. It began hacking on the back of Dustin's neck. Warm, semi-solid mucus splattered on his skin and dripped down the back of his shirt.

"Dreaming, yeah. It's all a dream. You know I dreamed? There were dreams of you. Of Mom. Mark. John. John killed me once already, you know? I'd already seen the other side. And then—it pushed down hard, causing Dustin to cry out again—I came back. You know what they say: 'I already died once, you can't die twice.' It's all just one big dream…"

Dustin had his eyes closed. He opened them now as the grip on his shoulder first let up and then was gone completely. He quickly turned his head in the opposite direction as he heard the crunching of dead corn stalks a few feet away from him. It had told him not to look at it, and now he had absolutely no desire to. Whatever it was that carried such a voice was not pure.

"Look now," it said, a little farther away now. "It's okay to look, p-p-p-promise, Dusty."

As if on rusty hinges, Dustin slowly turned his head. Nothing in front of him but the tangerine-tinted corn stalks and sunflower plants. Somewhere not too far beyond where he was there was a faint rustling sound; he could see the sunflower heads above him moving along with it.

"We're going on an adventure tonight," Trevor's Marge Simpson voice called from somewhere in the corn. "Taking Mom's car, just like the good ol' days. A little joy ride. You remember those, bro?"

"Y-y-y-yeah." Dustin almost sounded like he was stuck in a loop, himself. "Yeah, I remember."

"Gooooood. Rest up, and be ready-ready-ready. Remember, it's a dream. Just like in Hell…Hell-Hell-Helly-Hell."

Dustin watched and listened as there were more cracks and the rustling of leaves. The patch of corn ahead of him moved and swayed. Soon, the noises were a distant echo, and then gone entirely. The corn was still now.

He let out a shuddering cry that wouldn't stop. He sank to his knees, hugging them to his chest with his arms. Eventually, he lay down in the grass and rolled over, shaking in the fetal position until he passed out. That's how Desta and Cindy found him a half an hour later.

CHAPTER 9

Desta drove frantically to UPMC Mercy in Pittsburgh. Dustin was awake, though he hadn't said a word. He just sat in the front seat of the car the entire time, staring ahead. He blinked occasionally, more from reflex than from feeling any conscious need to do so. Cindy had given them a pair of jeans for Dustin to change into before they left. Desta ended up having to change him in the bathroom. He would put his hands on her shoulders to support himself when prompted; he lifted his legs at the right times to take the old pants off and put the new ones on. But beyond that, nothing.

They arrived at the hospital around an hour after leaving the ranch. Dustin had gotten out of the car just fine. He'd walked with her through the parking lot to the ER entrance, sat in one of the chairs in the lobby, waited while she gave the receptionist his insurance information and got him registered in without a word. When the nurse came out twenty minutes later to take him back, Dustin obliged willingly, that vacant, glazed-over look on his face all the while.

They checked his eyes, his reflexes, and his vitals. Everything seemed to be in perfect working order, besides the fact that he didn't even attempt to blink when the doctor had shone the bright light directly into his pupils. Desta thought of a robot, or the pod people from the *Invasion of the Body Snatchers*. It was like her perfect boy had left her and was replaced by some barely functioning drone, her real son still wandering the cornfield, lost, afraid, searching for her.

"So, what do you think?" she asked as Dustin lay on the bed beside her. She'd considered taking the doctor outside to ask this question, but it didn't matter—Dustin couldn't hear them, anyway.

"It could be a variety of things," he said while looking over his clipboard. "A seizure episode, some kind of sudden shock. I don't see it in my notes here. Has Dustin ever been diagnosed with epilepsy?"

"No-n-n-no, nothing even close to that. He has a few allergies. Peanuts, hay fever." A light bulb switched on in her head. "We were at my friend's ranch in Somerset when this happened. He'd been riding horses, hanging out in the barn. You don't think—"

"No," the doctor cut her off, setting his clipboard on the desk beside him. "Even if he, say, came in contact with peanuts or something that would make him have a severe allergic reaction, it wouldn't cause this. To be honest, Mrs. Taylor—"

"*Ms.* Taylor. My husband passed away a long time ago."

"Okay, Ms. Taylor. I'm not sure what caused Dustin to be in the state he's in. I'd like to keep him at least overnight to re-evaluate him and rule out all possibilities." He stopped for a moment, clearing his throat. "Again, I don't see it in my notes. Ms. Taylor, has your son ever been treated for any psychiatric issues?"

Desta looked at him with her head cocked, uncomprehending.

"Psychiatric issues? Like what?"

"Borderline Personality Disorder, Manic Depressive Disorder, things like that?"

"Oh, no," she said immediately. "Nothing like that. We did have him seeing someone at Family Services down where we live for a couple of years after his older brother died, but that was it."

The doctor raised an eyebrow. "Older brother died? When did that happen?"

"Six years ago. He and Dustin were almost inseparable for that last year. He…was a drug addict. He exposed Dustin to a lot of things he shouldn't have seen. He was only eleven."

The doctor had his clipboard in his hand again, writing quickly.

"And how did Dustin react to that initially?"

She looked at the boy on the table and felt her heart pang.

"Actually, almost just like this. Near catatonic, non-verbal. I had to dress him every day, take him to the bathroom. We were very scared."

"I'm sure. I'm sorry you both had to go through that. Being at your friend's ranch, do you think there was anything there that could have triggered this? Something that may have reminded him of that time and what happened?"

Desta put a finger to her chin and thought hard. Trevor *had* been to Cindy's house a long time ago to ride horses, but there was nothing there that would alert Dustin to this fact, let alone cause his mind to revert back to such a state. They'd had a completely different stable when Trevor was there. It had burnt down ten years ago and was rebuilt in a different location. Cindy had stopped inviting them after their last visit. That's whenever Trevor had started to slip.

"No," Desta finally said. "Nothing."

"Hmmm." The doctor thought to himself. "Okay, we'll keep him here tonight for observation. It's not very comfortable, but you're more than welcome to stay with him after he's admitted. We can get him a room with a second open bed so you can get some sleep."

"Thank you, I appreciate that."

The doctor nodded. He wrote a final note on the clipboard and left the room.

Desta and Dustin sat alone for a while, her looking at him, him looking at the big Stop Smoking poster ahead, but really looking at nothing at all.

"Baby, I'm so sorry. So, so sorry." Desta had her head in her hands, weeping, unknowing what to do. Somehow, some-way, this had been all her fault. If she lost him…if he were truly gone, it would completely shatter her. She had no one else in the world. A second failure with one of her sons was something she could not handle.

"Mom? Are you okay?"

She instantly put her head up. Dustin had turned in her direction, his expression confused and scared. His one hand was clenching and unclenching around his neck—a mannerism he hadn't exhibited since he was a little boy.

"Dustin, baby? Can you hear me?"

"Yeah," he said groggily." What are we doing here? You on your period?"

It took everything within her when she stood up to hug him and not land one upside the back of his head instead. She held him closely against her breast, stroking his hair, whis-pering in his ear. He initially put up some resistance, then gave in and leaned into her, hugging her back.

"Dustin, what happened? What happened out there?" She let go, giving him space to talk.

"I…" he started.

"Yeah, honey, take your time."

"Had a bad dream. I was at the cornfield, looking at the sunflowers. They use them to, you know, hold the corn stalks up."

Desta nodded fervently. "Yeah, sweetie, I know." She

64

hadn't used pet names for him in a very long time. They felt almost foreign rolling off her tongue. Foreign, but right.

"And then, I started…dreaming. Something was there with me, in the cornfield. It talked to me and said things to me. Really bad things." He rubbed his left shoulder.

"Uh-huh. What kind of things did it say to you?"

"It said," Dustin began to say, and then that blank look washed over his face again. Desta panicked, getting ready to snap her fingers in front of his eyes, but then he blinked and was back with her. "I don't remember. I was out in the sun for a while and didn't drink water. I remember feeling really hot. Do you think that's what happened? Maybe heat stroke?"

She looked into his eyes closely. She knew when he was lying. She knew he'd been lying about needing a fan from the storage room the other day, the same way she knew that he was telling the truth when he said someone had broken in that same night. What she was seeing right now was like an amalgamation of the two: truthful Dustin and lying Dustin. He wasn't intentionally being deceptive with her, but he wasn't exactly telling her the whole story, either. Desta had never seen that look on his face before. Strange, but he was also only minutes removed from coming out of some psychiatric trance. It made sense that he would be a bit disoriented.

"Okay, baby. I'll have them get the doctor and tell them to bring you some Gatorade. Are you still feeling hot or sick?" She looked at his complexion. He did seem a bit red—probably from a combination of riding like he had been and being passed out in the open sun for who knew how long. Heat stroke made complete sense since it had been an unseasonably warm day, especially at the end of November in southwestern Pennsylvania. An Indian Summer, they called it.

"Yeah," Dustin said. "Have them bring me two Gatorades, if you can. Get a third if you want to have a chugging context. Cindy told me about you and beer pong back in college."

Again, Desta resisted the urge to slap him and went to tell

the nurse that Dustin was alert and thirsty. They brought his Gatorades, followed by the doctor returning twenty minutes later. He examined Dustin and said he seemed fine, but still suggested he stay through the night for evaluation.

"Mom, I just want to go home. I feel so tired and just want to sleep. I feel better now after the Gatorade, I promise."

Desta looked to the doctor.

"I mean, he's physically okay and cognitively responding to everything the way he should be. I'd suggest keeping an eye on things and following up with his PCP, ASAP. And go to an ER immediately if the symptoms return, okay, guys?"

They both acquiesced and waited for the nurse to give them their discharge papers. After that was done, they signed out and began the two and a half hour drive home. Neither of them talked, and there was no music—a rarity when both of them were in the car together, especially for a long drive such as this one.

Dustin didn't take his phone out one time, opting to use his hoodie from the back as a pillow and sleep against the passenger window. They arrived home near midnight and immediately went to both of their respective bedrooms, not even bothering to say good night to one another. Both were asleep within fifteen minutes after arrival. Dustin's nightmare was almost forgotten by then. He was ready to erase it completely with the introduction of new dreams, hopefully of the non-ghoulish, non-emotionally paralyzing variety.

As they fell asleep, a low *click* could be heard coming from the carport in front of the house. Slowly, the back hatch ascended, descending again moments later. A rattling of car keys blended in with the hum of the street lights above—the spare set Desta kept in the end table beside the couch. The beeping of the alarm being engaged was not heard, as it was unnecessary. The car would be leaving again very shortly.

CHAPTER 10

TAP! TAP! TAP, TAP! TAP!

Dustin awoke, groggy and unknowing where he was at first. He checked the time on his phone. 2:35 AM. He remembered being at the hospital, but everything before and after that was a complete blur. Something about a cornfield, and voices. One younger voice that had been weathered but still youthful, and another one that had been aged and destroyed well beyond its years. There was something else…rides. Horse rides, *joy* rides.

TAP, TAP, TAP!

He looked around, trying to locate the source of the noise. His bedroom door again? Had the junkie returned?

TAP, TAP TAP, TAP!

No, this wasn't coming from anywhere *inside* of the house; it sounded too muffled. He listened closely.

His window, something pinging off the glass. Still half asleep, Dustin stood up and walked over, leaning against the air conditioner and looking out. Beyond the dark outlines of some bushes and trees across the street, he could see nothing.

TAP!

He saw it this time. A small white pebble, aimed directly

at his window. He looked over the area again, but everything below was pitch black. He reached over and turned on his Steelers lamp. The faces of past greats like Terry Bradshaw and Jerome Bettis glowed into life as he continued to search, but the glare of the lamp against the window made outside visibility even more impossible.

Yawning and thinking he was dreaming, Dustin slipped his shoes on and went out of the room into the hallway. The space under Trevor's door was dark, just as it had been for the past six-plus years, minus the exception of one night. No worries. In a dream, the innocuous could mean everything, and the more eventful parts could mean absolutely nothing. It's just how dreams work.

This particular one was uncharacteristically vivid. He could feel the chill of the cold night air hit his face as he stepped outside. The crickets temporarily ceased in their loud chirping when he closed the door behind him. Halfway zombified, Dustin made his way down the front steps and looked around. Nothing. For a dream, this was pretty lame. At least Freddy Krueger could jump out at him from the side of the house, spice things up a little bit.

He heard a *clicking* noise. Turning around, he could see all the interior lights of the Civic lit up through the windshield. Feeling as if he were floating through the air, Dustin went to the car and opened the passenger door.

"No, little bro," a dirt-clogged voice said from somewhere in the back. "You drive now. Drive-drive-drive-drive-drive."

He looked over, seeing Mom's spare set of keys sitting on the front seat. Nodding as if it made complete sense, Dustin gently closed the door and made his way around the front to the driver's side. This time, the crickets did not stop chirping at the noise he was making. It was as if he belonged with them now, with the night.

He picked up the keys and slid into the driver's seat. He yawned, then placed them in the ignition.

"Turn the lights off first. Put it in reverse and coast it back before you turn it on. That way you don't wake-wake-wake Mom-Mom-Mom."

Dustin remembered Trevor's old routine for stealing the car well. Lights off, coast back into the street, turn the ignition, lights back on, and then cruise. It was ingrained within him the same way a balding forty-year-old might remember how to ride a bike despite having not been on one since they were a youth.

He performed every action with extreme precision, making sure the car was a good distance away from the house before putting it in park and switching it on. Some sane part of his mind told him to run back in the house and get his wallet with his learner's permit in it, but he ignored it. What were the cops going to do: give him a dream ticket that he would have to appear in dream court to pay a dream fine? The dream pigs could shove their dream ticket right up their dream asses.

Dustin put the car into drive and went slowly down Center Street. As he hit the first stop sign, he heard a rustling noise in the back. He looked towards the rear view to catch a glimpse of his riding companion, only to discover it had been pushed the whole way up so it was pointed at the roof of the Civic.

"Sorry, little bro. Still can't s-s-see me. I don't look so hot these days." The voice was closer to him now, inches from the back of his neck. His skin was covered in gooseflesh as he felt hot breath tickle the cilia in his ear.

"It's okay," Dustin said, "I forgot to comb my hair before I came out."

A loud choking noise erupted from the back, accompanied by the sound of a fist being pounded against one of the seats. It took almost twenty seconds of this for Dustin to realize what he was hearing wasn't choking at all; it was laughter. It was *laughing* at him.

"That's good, Mr. Mommy Man, really, really good. I bet you get *all* the bitches now. Just beat that pussy right the hell up!"

Dustin nodded, not knowing what to say. He'd made out with a girl under the bleachers at a football game last year, but then her father had caught them and pulled her away. He didn't even have a chance to get to second base.

"Where are we going?" Dustin said in a heavy voice. "We going to see Mark and John?"

It let out another choking laugh and slapped the back of Dustin's headrest, causing him to jolt in his seat.

"I don't think you want to go where they are, at least not yet-yet-yet. I-I-I-I just want to catch up. So, how've you been? How's Mom, Mr. Mommy-Man-Man-Man?"

"She's okay. Working really hard. She's a manager now. At the diner she used to work at before you, well, you know."

"I am *so* happy to hear that! And how about you? Still making good grades, going to school, licking Mom's coochie every time she spreads her legs?"

He could hear a gurgling noise coming from behind him. Moments later, a smell followed it. He recognized it instantly: St. Ives. It really was like old times.

"They opened up a liquor store right near the cemetery," it said as if reading Dustin's mind. "They got the *good* shit there."

Dustin looked up as he drove. The street lights were less blurred and more focused now. Also, he was becoming more alert to his surroundings. He could hear the car's motor rev when he pushed his foot against the accelerator, could feel himself being pushed slightly backward as momentum halted when he stopped at a light or a sign. More and more, he was awakening to the very real possibility that what he was experiencing may not be a dream at all. And if that were true, then that meant...

"What the fuck are you doing, bitch boy? Put it in drive before a cop notices or somethin'."

Dustin looked up. The traffic light he was stopped at had turned green. He hit the gas a little harder than he meant to. Both occupants of the car slammed against their seats as it lurched forward.

"*Daaaaaamn!* Little bro grew some nuts, after all. You better get a hold on that before the driving test-test-test. Mommy'll be taking you to your track meets for the rest of your life." More of that awful laughter, followed by the guzzling of St. Ives.

"Uh, yeah. How have you been, Trevor?" This is the first time he called it by name, mostly because he had now talked himself into the delusion that this was still a dream, despite every waking bit of reality around him pointing to the contrary.

"Oh," it said, " a little this, a little that. I've been having a good-good-good time. I see Grandma's still the snooping cunt she always was-was-was. Bitch almost got her throat slit a couple times the other night. Probably bleeds like cherry pie-pie-pie."

He was in the house during the day!? his mind screamed, followed by a reminder that this was all a dream, and there-fore anything said in this dream had no bearing on real life or anything that had occurred in it.

But the X-Box…the ring on the table.

THIS ISN'T REAL! STOP IT!

Dustin switched on the blinker and made a right onto Donegal, cruising right by the police station. He almost screamed as something cold and wet was suddenly pressing against the front of his shirt. Not wanting to, he looked down. The brown liquid of a half-drunk St. Ives was splashing around the glass of the bottle.

"Hit it," Trevor said in exactly the same tone it had used

all those years ago. This was not up for negotiation; Dustin was drinking it, whether he liked it or not.

Leaving his left hand on the wheel, Dustin reached up with his right and gripped the middle of the bottle. Cold condensation made his fingers come awake as he inched it between his legs and started undoing the cap. A small pocket of air was released with a loud *hisssss*. He looked down. Chunks of dirt were floating on top of the beer. From Trevor's mouth.

"What's the matter, pussy? Too scared?"

"No. I...just don't want to get a DUI, Trev. You remember when you got one. You had to do community service for six months."

Cold, bony fingers were suddenly wrapped around the front of Dustin's throat. He gagged and tried to cough as a flaky thumb pressed hard into his Adam's apple.

"You think you're fuckin' b-b-better than me-me-me? Drink it. Now."

Choking, Dustin raised the bottle to his mouth and took a big gulp. The fingers relinquished their grip as what felt like a solid brick squeezed through his swollen airway, inching through his chest with a painful thunk. An immediate sense of euphoria hummed through his body as he took a second hit, and then a third.

"*HEY!*" Trevor rasped at him. "Don't be drinking all my shit! I only scored-scored-scored a couple-couple. Double trouble, supple bubble. *YUM!*"

Dustin capped the bottle and passed it back. An unseen hand took it from him. He was going down Orchard now, driving 20 miles per hour over the speed limit. This was the street Mom took him on to practice parallel parking some-times. Now both sides were packed with cars, their owners having not woken up yet to get to work and start the day. He looked at the radio in the center console. 3:09 AM.

"Trev, can we go back? Mom's gonna be awake soon, and I

have a job interview at noon. Need to get some sleep." In all the chaos, he'd forgotten about the interview at Burger King he'd set up last week.

"Make a left first. We need to make a little-a little-a little-a little stop."

Dustin did as he was told, making a left at the stop sign between Orchard and Oakmont. He remembered this route well.

"Are we going to John's old house? You know it's not there anymore after the, um, explosion. They condemned it and tore it down." Dustin was trying to keep his tone as casual as possible. His throat hurt after being choked. Dreams weren't supposed to let you feel pain.

"Just keep driving," Trevor said.

They cruised slowly down Oakmont. Soon, they passed by a vacant lot that had a lone bench in the middle of it.

"Remember, little bro. You were s-s-supposed to be there that night. Mom was being a cunt and wouldn't let-let-let you go-go. I was gonna pick you up later. G-g-g-g-guess God had different plans."

Loud chugging commenced. Dustin's stomach churned. He ran his tongue along his upper front teeth, feeling a gritty residue on them. From Trevor's mouth. The lips of a dead person.

They moved on past the lot until they hit the end of the street, where the pavement looped around in a crescent. In the middle of the wraparound was a short dirt road that led to an opening in the woods beyond.

"Keep going, bitch boy. Just a little further."

"I wanna go home," Dustin pleaded. "Please, Trevor, let me go home. I don't like this."

"We-we-we are-are-are going home, buddy. You'll really like it. Promise."

Dustin drove through the woods. He was wide awake now, watching as the beams lit up the trees on both sides of him. The scene was surreal. He wasn't *supposed* to be here, out in the dark at this time of night. He was supposed to be at home in bed, eyes closed shut until Mom banged on his door in the morning. Normal things, safe things. That's what he was *supposed* to be doing.

"Stop. Right before the river. You're gonna love this, bro."

Dustin stopped and put the car in park. He had a brief glimpse of the sparkling waters of the Allegheny River before he cut the lights and turned the car off. Now everything was completely dark; not even the trees could be seen. The only sounds that could be heard were his shallow breaths and the deep, raspy wheezing blowing directly into his ear. Trevor could have kissed him on the cheek if he wanted to.

"Get out. And don't turn around-round-round-gray bloodhound. Just keep walkin'."

Dustin opened the door and got out, walking down the dirt path until he reached the edge of the river. It was still tonight, the sound of the running water barely audible over the owls and crickets surrounding them.

My people now Dustin thought. *Maybe my people forever. I'm going to die here, and no one will ever know. Except Trevor. But who's he gonna tell?*

"Lay down on the ground. On your smelly-smelly-smelly little belly."

When Dustin didn't comply, the thing that was once Trevor put a hand on the back of his head and kicked its foot forward. With a thud, Dustin landed face-first in the mud. He gasped for air as a worm passed through his nasal passage into the back of his throat. His gag reflex was instantly triggered. He retched, vomiting up the three mouthfuls of St. Ives from earlier. He screamed as he felt the front of a boot connect with his sternum. Timberlands. Some far-off part of him remembered that Trevor had been buried in those.

"That's how you-you-you repay me for hooking you-you-you up!? Puking my shit up!? I coulda been on paper for that, mother-

fucker. Caught a case!" It wound back and kicked Dustin again, knocking the wind out of him. *"I-I-I WENT-WENT-WENT OUT OF MY WAY FOR YOU! I ALWAYS DID!"*

Not giving Dustin time to catch his breath, it dropped down suddenly and grabbed his head, shoving it into the Allegheny. Loud splashes were heard as Trevor held him under, occasionally cut by Dustin's intermittent screams as he pushed himself up, trying to get air.

The Trevor-thing was strong, impossibly strong. It fought back with a vigor that Dustin had never seen when it was alive. Soon, his body gave up fight. Using all of his reserves, he managed to get his head up one last time, taking in a big breath of air and holding it before he was submerged again. After a while, he stopped moving. Trevor pulled him out and flipped him on his back.

"Look at the stars, little bro. Look at *him*."

Trevor let him lie there a minute. When it decided it had been long enough, it pinched Dustin's nose shut with its fingers and inhaled deeply. It leaned over, a shadow amongst the shadows. It parted what was left of its lips and pressed them against its brother's, blowing deeply.

As it did this, Dustin's eyes suddenly shot open. He bit down on Trevor's lower lip, causing it to howl out in pain. Using all of his might, he threw his knee up, catching it square in the groin. He felt the weight roll off him to the ground. Seizing the opportunity, he twisted his body until he was on his belly, frantically clawing at the mud until his hands found traction and he was able to push himself up.

"DUSTIN!" Its voice did not sound like Trevor or even human anymore. It was both high-pitched and guttural at the same time, a voice that had existed since before the beginning of forever. Demonic.

"LITTLE BROTHER! COME BACK! SEE ME! SEE ME!"

Dustin stumbled up the incline to the Civic. He'd left the

driver's side door open. He flung himself in and immediately began fumbling with the ignition.

"DUSTIIIIIIIIN! DUSTIIIIIIIIIIN!"

It was making its way through the mud and grass. Dustin could hear its plodding footsteps growing closer and closer. His fingers found purchase on the keys and turned. The Civic puttered into life. The thing was banging on the hood now, the pounding of its fists against the fiberglass sounding like a shaman playing a war theme on African tribal drums. Soon, the pounding was changing directions, growing closer.

THE LOCKS! SHIT!

Dustin's left hand flew over to the console on the door. The lights were still switched off, and he didn't have time to turn them on. He pressed a button and heard a mechanical whirl, followed by a cold breeze blowing on his neck.

FUCK! THE WINDOW!

He pressed again. The breeze was cut off.

"BROTHERRRRRR!"

His fingers dropped down two buttons and pushed. A light *click* from all four sides. He felt his door reverberating against his arm as whatever was inhabiting Trevor's body found the handle and tried to pull. Seeing it was locked out, it began slamming itself into the door. Dustin felt the car rocking against the ground, the force increasing with each subsequent hit.

He threw the transmission into reverse and slammed on the gas, praying the wheels were straight enough that he wouldn't hit a tree behind him. The Civic's tires kicked up mud and rocks as it sped back through the tiny opening. The pounding on the exterior soon stopped. Dustin remembered in the silence to switch the headlights on.

What he saw standing on the dirt road ahead of him made liquid ice pump through his veins. It was only just a glimpse, a quick trick of the eyes that wasn't a trick at all but some ghastly truth of existence that not even the greatest of illusions could replicate.

Its body was charcoal black, emaciated to the point he could probably wrap both of his hands around its torso and have his fingers touch. It was wearing a pair of Trevor's old clothes: a purple Tupac shirt, and a pair of tan cargo shorts. *All Eyez on Me*, the text on the shirt read. It must have dug those out while going through the storage totes. They had been baggy on Trevor in even the healthiest of days. Now, the fabric hung off of his brittle frame as if someone had dropped a deflated hot air balloon on top of it.

The corpse looked like a black widow spider that had been genetically mutated to take on the height and semi-appearance of a human being. The worst, though, was its face. Oh, God…its face.

The majority of Trevor's dirty blond hair was still there, though some had been ripped out in large patches. The skin on the right side of its face was gone in sections, exposing skull and the piece of orbital bone Dustin had seen in the casket all those years ago. Looking closely, he could see its complexion was not all black but dark purple and green in places. Its eyelids were completely gone, leaving two white, bloodless orbs to perpetually peer out at him as he peeled back towards the road. That was the worst part of it all: it wasn't moving as if to do something; it wasn't giving chase in an attempt to catch up to the car. It was just standing there in between the trees, looking directly at him with those eyes that had been driven imperceptibly mad from the sights they'd beheld on the other side.

The car hit the gravel. Dustin quickly spun it around. He could no longer see the thing. Not wanting to give it a chance to catch up, he put the car into drive and raced back down Oakmont at 55 miles per hour. Fuck the neighbors, fuck the laws, and fuck the cops. What he'd just seen wasn't human; what inhabited it wasn't from this world. Maybe it had been once, but death had taken whatever good parts remained of Trevor's soul and sucked them all out, putting the godless remainder back into the decaying husk he was running from now.

He came up to the turn onto Donegal and took it on screeching tires, uncaring of the big red sign telling him to stop. All the way like that, he drove home on the residential streets and alleyways. Twice, he almost t-boned cars on their way to work, not even attempting to brake before or after the near-collisions.

He didn't stop until he turned into the driveway of the house, where he slammed the brakes on and put the car into park. He grabbed the keys and jumped out, pressing the lock button five or six times. The quiet block became temporarily alive with the squawking of the alarm beeping over and over again.

Not looking back, Dustin ran up the stairs to the front door. He slammed it shut and engaged both the deadbolt lock and the one on the knob. That done, he went through the entire house, rechecking the window latches, the lock on the back door in the kitchen, the basement door leading outside, and then the front door again.

When that was done, he went to his bedroom and threw off his muddy clothes, replacing them with the plaid pajama set Mom had gotten him for Christmas last year. Then, he went through and checked all the locks again, pulling on the doors and windows as hard as he could to make sure they wouldn't open. Not that it mattered; Trevor was strong, possessing a supernatural energy that was fueled by something far beyond this realm. If Dustin hadn't taken that breath before it held him under the water, hadn't caught it by surprise...

Dustin began to shiver uncontrollably. He was in the living room now. He looked to the X-Box controller sitting on the arm of the couch. That *thing* had touched it when it changed his username. Unthinking, he snatched it up and took it to the kitchen, where he dumped it in the trash. *It* had also touched his clothes, his hair, his skin, his lips...

He would burn the clothes tomorrow, then take the longest, hottest shower that he had ever taken in his entire life. Every fiber in his being was screaming to do that now, to wash every trace of the entity's touch off of him, but he couldn't do it—he was barely able to stand, exhausted beyond words. He would need to remain tainted for at least a few more hours, getting clean after he rested, after the dream was finally over.

Not knowing what else to do, Dustin went to the only place in the world where he could feel safe at that moment in time. As quietly as he could, he padded down the hallway and pushed open the first door on the right. There was no need to turn the knob first—it was always open for him.

He tip-toed his way inside and lay down on the floor beside the bed. He stayed like that, trembling and chattering his teeth as the soothing snores above him went on uninterrupted. Like the crickets, like the owls, like the river. He belonged with them now, but he also belonged with *her*. Mom. His one and only true protector in the entire world.

CHAPTER 11

D ustin snapped awake, screaming while holding his arms across his chest. Desta jumped back in reaction. She was still wearing her nightgown. The shock of his state caused her to forget this fact, and her left breast became clearly visible as the string on her shoulder slipped down. She immediately pulled it up, hoping Dustin was still asleep enough not to have noticed.

She herself had only woken up five minutes ago. She was attempting to get out of bed and put her slippers on to go pee when she had almost stepped directly on his head. He was lying on the bare hardwood, no pillow, no blanket. A fear had crossed her mind that he'd had another episode like the one yesterday. His terrified scream seconds ago was like music to her ears.

"Dustin, baby, what happened?"

The finger indentations on his neck became immediately apparent as he moved his head. His hair was matted together, and his forehead and hands were streaked with dirt. She could see his eyes were bloodshot, his skin a ghostly white.

"Mom...Mom...*MOMMY!*" Dustin immediately began

bawling upon seeing her. Tears streamed down his cheeks, causing slivers of peach to show through the dirt.

Desta dropped to her knees and wrapped him in her arms, rocking him and shushing him as she had when he was a baby. He allowed her to do this, letting his full weight fall on her shoulders. Normally, her slender frame wouldn't be up for such a task, but now she was able to support him with nearly zero effort.

"Baby, baby, baby…hey, it's okay, I'm here. I promise. Just calm down, everything's okay. You're safe now, okay?"

Dustin nodded into her shoulder, leaving light brown smudges on her white nightgown. She leaned down, kissing his forehead and rocking him some more. He hugged her even tighter, sniffling lightly and trying to pull himself together.

"He…he…"

"Who, baby? Who did this to you?"

"Him-him-him. He-he-he…" Dustin remembered Trevor's dead voice, how it would repeat itself like its mind was caught in a loop before it righted itself again. He pressed his face against her bare shoulder and muffled a scream.

"Shh, shh. You don't have to tell me right now. You stay right here. I'm not going anywhere."

She reached up, fumbling around on the bed until she found her phone. She brought it down, opening it and searching through her contacts. She found the one listed as Work and dialed it, pressing the phone to her ear.

"Sheila, it's Desta. I need to not come in today, family emergency. Wha—no, no, everything is okay. Dustin had an… accident. No, he's fine, but he needs me here. Uh-huh, okay. I'll give you a call later. Thanks so much, honey. Mmm, bye." She put the phone down as Dustin clung to her, running her fingers through his hair.

"Mom, mom, mom. I'm s-s-s-sorry…I-I-I—"

"You don't have to say anything," she said soothingly. "

You want me to make you some hot cocoa?" This had always been a sure-fire method to get him to calm down when he was younger.

"Yeah. Yes, if you can, please."

Desta had to practically pry him off of her to stand up. A part of her didn't want to do it, yearning to be there and hold him for as long as possible, but she had to make sure he didn't fall into another catatonic state again. Still, it pained her to release contact.

"Okay. You think maybe take a shower, get your head clear? I'll have cocoa and breakfast out for when you get done."

"Okay. Yeah. Yeah, that sounds good."

She held a hand out and helped pull him to his feet— again, an otherwise impossible task in ordinary circumstances. She walked him to the bathroom, picking out a fresh towel and washcloth for him to use. She asked if he wanted her to get some clothes from his room. He nodded as he took off his pajama top and started brushing his teeth. She did a double-take before she left the bathroom. While observing him, she noticed how long and hard he was brushing.

"Sweetie, you'll make your gums bleed. That's enough."

He looked over to her, a line of white foam dripping from the right side of his mouth.

"Eah. O-ay, 'Om," he said through the toothpaste.

"Okay, good."

She went to his room and picked out boxers, a pair of socks, black Nike shorts, and his orange Bob Marley shirt. Dustin didn't even attempt to match his clothes half the time. Left to his own devices, he wouldn't even wear the correct pair of socks. So many mornings, he'd walk out for school only for Desta to immediately send him back to his room to change. She cherished the moments when she could fold Dustin's laundry or choose his clothes for him.

She went back into the bathroom and set the folded outfit

on top of the laundry basket. He was already in the shower with the curtain drawn. She could hear the water splashing off his body onto the plastic of the curtain and the wall on the other side. The room was already filled with steam. She walked by the mirror and tried to look at herself, but all she could see was a foggy gray cloud.

Desta changed into a plain black t-shirt and a pair of Pink jogging pants, then proceeded to the kitchen to make breakfast and Dustin's cocoa.

Bacon sizzled loudly in a skillet as the Keurig brewed a pod of cocoa into an extra-large coffee mug. While everything was being made, Desta noticed her phone battery was only on 15%. She remembered that she'd left her charger in the car. She finished the bacon and set it on a plate beside the other one holding the scrambled eggs. Then, she grabbed her keys from the counter and ran outside to the car. When she caught sight of the state of it, her mouth ran dry.

The front of the white Civic was covered in dusty hand and boot prints. Desta went to the side, seeing those same markings on the front driver's door, along with large dents all through the shell. She unlocked the car and pushed her upper half inside. The smell of stale beer hit her nostrils immediately. Supporting herself on the seat's headrest, she leaned over and inspected the back. A half-drunk bottle of St. Ives malt liquor lay on the floor. The plastic mat underneath it was covered in the same boot tread markings as the exterior. Someone had been sitting back there.

Desta grabbed her charger from the center console and made her way back into the house. The previously pleasant aromas of bacon and steaming cocoa were nauseating to her now. She choked back a throat full of bile as she transitioned from the living room to the kitchen. Dustin was in there now at the table, hungrily taking down his breakfast. He was wearing the fresh clothes she had picked out for him; his hair was damp and springy from the shower. He looked up at her when she entered. The color had come back into his face, but the vessels in his eyes were still zig-zags of pure red.

"You feeling better?"

"Yeah, a little bit. Thank you, Mom. I think I might call Burger King today and reschedule that interview. So tired." He picked up the mug with both hands and took a big sip.

Desta sat down across from him and watched while he ate. He seemed oblivious, in a world all of his own. He was setting the mug directly on the table, no coaster. Twice, half of the eggs he picked up with his fork fell to the floor between his feet. He made no effort to catch them or pick them up after the fact.

Zombie. Robot. Pod person. Trevor.

Desta's mind said the thought before she could stop it. Now that the cat was out of the bag, she couldn't help but notice the direct parallels between Dustin's behavior for the past few days and his late brother's, especially during the last two years before his death.

Dustin finished breakfast and took his plate to the sink. He dropped it right in, not even attempting to spray it off as he normally would. It was as if he was going through the motions of what his normal routine would be, but didn't have the mental capacity to worry about the fine details. It took everything within her not to yell at him, to scream that he needed to clean up after himself and make sure everything was tidy. He wasn't thinking clearly…that was it. She would just have to make everything right again, like she always did. He needed her.

She waited until he sat back down at the table. The marks on his neck stood out prominently. With all the dirt washed away, they now looked a dark purple rather than red. Dustin was looking down while wringing his hands. The knuckles were scraped and raw. His fingernails had dirt embedded underneath them.

"Dustin," Desta said slowly.

"Yeah?" He didn't look up.

"Did you take my car? While I was sleeping last night?" The words came out like acid burning a hole through her tongue. A flashback played in her mind from seven years ago, sitting in this same room, saying the same words to Trevor. She had found the same car in a similar state, covered in mud with dents all through the exterior. Luckily, a mechanic friend had been able to pop most of those out for her. How it was now…she might not be so lucky.

Dustin fixated on his scabbed knuckles. He was biting his lip, another behavior he hadn't indulged in since he was a child. Before, it was an indicator that he was holding something back. Or lying.

"I'm not going to ask again, Dustin. Did you take my car out, and if so, where did you go?"

"Yes, ma'am," he said quietly. "I took the car last night. He made me do it. He woke me up. I thought I was dreaming."

Desta examined Dustin closely. While his eyes were still downcast, he wasn't biting his lip anymore. Not lying, no. Scared, scared beyond his ability to convey what he was even scared of. A mother always knows.

"You don't look good, honey. I'm going to get some air in here."

Desta jumped and screamed a little. Dustin had his hand wrapped around her wrist like an iron vice. He wasn't hurting her, but she also wasn't going anywhere until he chose to let her go.

"Don't open the windows or the doors!" His tone wasn't harsh, just filled with fear. "Please," he begged, tears on the rims of his eyes.

She sat back down.

"Okay, okay, I won't open anything. But you have to let go of me, okay?"

Visions of different mind-altering substances rolled through Desta's mind like car parts on an assembly line belt.

Marijuana, cocaine, methamphetamine, heroin, little blue and pink pills, mushrooms. Could drug-induced delusion and paranoia happen so severely and so quickly? She had dabbled when she was a teen and in her early twenties, but never in large quantities and never for a prolonged period of time. She had known very quickly with Trevor. He had already possessed an explosive personality that made his use very hard to hide. But Dustin was naturally predisposed to be easygoing and mellow. All it took was one wrong person, one wrong move to become instantly hooked.

Thoughts of John Brennegan waiting in her driveway for Trevor came to mind, and now it was her biting her own bottom lip to quell the ominous dread building inside of her. It was happening again. As hard as she had tried to maintain a sense of normalcy and protect Dustin, he too was being pulled into the same cycle all over again. She couldn't lose him. *Wouldn't* lose him.

Dustin did as she asked, releasing her wrist. She breathed a deep sigh of relief.

"I went into my car to get my charger," she said. "There's mud all over it. It reeks of beer in there. I found the bottle in the back."

Dustin mumbled something.

"What did you say?"

He spoke up. "It's not beer; it's malt liquor. The kind Trevor used to drink."

Now the dread was morphing into something much worse. She remembered leaving for work in the mornings to find mounds of empty bottles all over the floor and backseat of the car, Trevor nowhere to be found.

At least Dustin came home, her mind tried to reassure her. At least you know he's alive. One of your boys is alive. That's what counts.

"Who choked you?"

"He did."

86

"Who?"

Dustin put a hand to his head. Headache. A hangover. That's what it was. History repeating itself all over again.

"I...can't tell you." He shook his head. "You wouldn't understand or probably believe me if I did."

"Dustin," Desta said, "if you don't tell me what happened, I'm calling the police. Someone already broke in my house. You were having damn *seizures* yesterday while I was visiting my friend. And now this? I don't know what you've gotten yourself into, but I'll be damned if I sit around and watch the same thing happen to you that happened to your brother. I won't do it." She crossed her arms, waiting for his response. She knew exactly what had happened—what she needed was for him to just come out and say it, to clear the air and make the truth finally known between the two of them. She hated it when they were dishonest with each other.

He swallowed a lump in his throat.

"You...won't believe me if I tell you. I really, really want to."

"Try me." Desta had learned to believe in a great many things as the years passed by.

He sighed.

"The same...*person* that broke into the house the other night did it again. He made me take your car to Laneville down by the river. He made me get out, and..."

Desta's hackles were raised now.

"And...what?"

"He tried to kill me, Mom!" Dustin said, starting to blubber. "He made me get out and lay on the ground. He choked me and kicked me, then he tried to drown me. I fought back. Kneed him in the di—he looked at her and his cheeks turned red—I kneed him. Then I drove back here as fast as I could. I don't know where he is now."

Desta was eyeing him closely, trying to spot any signs of deception. There were none.

"And what did he look like?"

His eyes shifted from hers. His bottom lip was tucked in his mouth again. Lying.

"I don't know," he finally said. "I only saw him once when I was pulling away from the river. He was all black. Not like a black guy, but like he was wearing sweats and a mask or something. All I saw were his eyes. They were…" He trailed off, staring out the window behind her. No more lip biting.

"His eyes were what? What about his eyes?" The dread was back now.

"Really, really white," Dustin finished. "Really white, and *wide*. So, so wide."

They sat there like that in silence for a long time. A hummingbird had flown up to the window at some point. It was still there, flittering its wings wildly, beak nearly hitting the glass, as if it was trying to get inside, away from something out there.

"Get your shoes. Then call Burger King and tell them you can't come in for your interview today." Desta was already on the move, collecting her keys and charger and dropping them in her purse.

"Where are we going?" he asked as he watched her zoom around the kitchen. "Mom, the cops aren't going to be able to find it—him. Trust me."

"We're not going to the cops. Now come on, hurry up while it's still early and there's nobody down there."

"Down *where?*" Dustin was in the foyer now, sliding his shoes on.

"'Down where?' Where do you think? The river, sweetie." All concern was gone from her voice now, replaced by a tone of steely determination and resolve.

Dustin was leaning against the wall, holding his side. The longer he was awake, the more he suspected the Trevor-thing may have bruised a rib or two. It hurt immensely to bend down, and walking left him wanting to sit after only a minute or two, not to mention the pains in his throat and shoulder. Like in life, everything Trevor had touched yesterday hurt.

Heavy footsteps came from Desta's room. She was in the hallway now, coming towards him with her hands on her hips. She'd put on a pair of old sneakers from when she tried to do Zumba a few years ago. Dustin didn't like the look on her face. It was the same one she'd have when he would spill orange juice on the counter, or when he'd stay up too late yelling at people on Call of Duty, or when someone cut her off in traffic. Desta was *pissed*.

"Let's go. We're taking care of this *right now*."

Without another word, Desta strode past him and out the front door. Dustin followed right behind her, but not before snatching his aluminum baseball bat from the foyer closet. He made sure the front door was locked with his keys and then got in the car. Desta didn't question his choice to bring the bat, and Dustin didn't offer an explanation. They put the car in reverse, then headed towards Laneville.

CHAPTER 12

Dustin called Burger King on the ride there. He explained to the manager that he had suffered some kind of medical episode the day before and had been advised by the doctor to stay at home and rest—not a lie in the slightest. The manager was very sympathetic and understanding.

"Not a problem at all, buddy. Just stay at home for a couple of days and rest up. We'll reschedule the interview for sometime next week when you're feeling more up to it. We got lots of slots to fill, so don't worry. We'll have something for ya."

Dustin thanked the man and hung up, praying he was telling the truth about them still having an opening next week. There was a new pair of Jordans coming out that he'd had his eye on ever since they were announced, plus a big metal festival coming to Wheeling in the Spring. Not that such things mattered when he'd just been abducted and almost murdered in the woods by a dead thing less than twelve hours ago. An image popped up in his mind of it standing in between the trees, caught in the headlights, unmoving, just staring at him. He shuddered from the thought.

Desta drove slightly slower than he had the night before, maintaining a steady 40 miles per hour compared to his 55. He could tell from that look on her face that she wanted to go faster, but was holding back, not wanting to get pulled over and be delayed from the mission at hand. What that mission was, exactly, Dustin didn't know, but he did know God help anything that stood in her way from accomplishing it.

No, God help her, he thought. *She has no idea what she's up against, if it's even still there.*

He had considered that maybe the Trevor-thing had come back during the night and stowed away in the car again somehow, but he'd made more than triple sure to lock it, plus he had the only set of spare keys in his nightstand. To his knowledge, they were safe, for now.

Dustin watched as they passed by the vacant lot again. There was an old man on a bench, feeding nuts to squirrels. Two women in spandex passed by them on their way to the river. It looked like they had just come from the path he and Mom were about to drive down. Had *it* still been there, watching from the bushes as they casually went about their morning, unaware of the evil lurking just a few feet away?

They reached the U in the road and drove down the dirt path in the center. The woods didn't seem so threatening in the daytime, whenever everything was bright and they weren't the only conscious human beings within a three-mile radius.

Looks can be deceiving, little bro. Trevor, *live* Trevor's voice was speaking in his head now. *I could be out here anywhere. Better visibility. Be on the lookout. I could pop out of nowhere and beat your bitch ass to a pulp, Mama's boy.*

The Civic finally reached the end of the trail. Dustin looked around everywhere, trying to spot the Trevor-thing or any remote sign that it might still be there. All was still. Birds flew from tree to tree, chirping merrily.

Looks can be deceiving, little bro.

"Give me that," Desta said, nodding towards the bat in his lap.

"Mom, I don't think—"

"*Give* me that," she said in a voice that said her command was not up for debate. He handed Desta the bat. She gripped the black taped handle and got out of the car. Dustin took a deep breath, cringing at the pain that shot through his ribs. Then, he followed her.

"Mom," he whispered. "Make sure it can't get inside."

Desta raised the fob in the air and pressed it twice, making the car beep so she knew the alarm was activated. Dustin ran back to the Civic and pulled the passenger door handle, just to make sure. When it didn't budge, he turned and rejoined Desta in the middle of the clearing.

"Be careful, Mom. It's really strong."

Not even registering (or caring) that Dustin kept referring to his assailant as an "it" rather than a he or a him, she approached the largest, thickest oak tree she could find. She aimed, wound the bat back, and slammed it as hard as she could into the trunk. A metallic *PING!* reverberated through the air. A flurry of birds above them took flight, flapping wildly into the blue sky, fleeing to a quieter place.

Dustin ran over and tried to grab the bat from here. His side was on fire now. The fear-induced adrenaline coursing through his body caused him not to notice.

"*Mom, no!*" he said as loudly as he could without breaking a whisper. "*What are you doing!?*"

"Listen here, you motherfucker!" Desta shouted at full volume. *"I'll say this once and only once: you stay the fuck away from my boy! You've had your fun, but it's over now! You come back around my house, my son, or me, you're gonna wish you were never fucking born! YOU HEAR ME!?"*

To emphasize her point, Desta wailed the bat into the tree over and over again until her hands ached from the reverberation.

Shaking, Dustin looked around and listened closely. Somewhere, far off in the distance, he heard the crackling of leaves and the snapping of tree branches. Whether they were footsteps or not, he could not tell. What he did know was that whatever it was was moving quickly, away from their location. He could understand why. In that moment, seeing Mom like that, hearing her as she was, he was just as—if not *more*—scared of her than he was of the creature he'd fought with in this same place just a few short hours ago.

Desta walked past him and tossed the bat in his hands.

"Come on. We're going home so you can get some sleep. I'll make you some more cocoa."

"Mom, what in the actual fu—"

"*I SAID COME ON!*"

Dustin hopped to, a mixture of his pain and her speed making it almost impossible for him to keep up. The birds above them had returned, as if nothing had happened. Like the crickets had acted with Trevor. Creatures of the night vs. those of the day. The crickets feared the birds and hid from them out of fear of being consumed. Did some part of Trevor remember her voice, what she could be like whenever she was pushed too far past her breaking point? The noises moving away from them seemed to say so, though Dustin had no way to confirm or deny that.

He finally caught up to his mom and slid into the seat beside her. He kept his eyes dead ahead as she pulled back, flashbacks playing in his mind of that bloated, deformed thing staring out at him. Somehow, the memory didn't have quite the same effect on him now as it had when they'd first arrived.

"Mom?" he asked hesitantly as they turned out of Laneville.

"Yes, sweetheart?" Her voice sounded pleasant enough, though a hint of that earlier fire was still there.

"That was fuckin' bad ass."

"Thanks, hon. I'd never let anyone hurt you."

"I know."

They went the rest of the way back to the house in a serene silence.

CHAPTER 13

Weeks went by after the day in the woods. Dustin went back to school, began working part-time at Burger King, and even asked a girl to go to the Winter Ball with him in December: Stacy Demeno. She wasn't the prettiest or most popular girl in school, but she was cute. More importantly than that, she was smart, regularly hitting honor roll every semester and toasting superficial hotties like Meghan Mullahan in debate class whenever they were paired off against one another.

The memory of the Trevor-thing lingered on, but with it came a sense of security as time passed by. A horrible thing had happened, yes, something that very few people had ever witnessed, if any. But as with anything else a human being experiences, life goes on, and we have to eventually learn to cope with and accept our traumas as a fact of reality. A reanimated corpse of the person who used to traumatize Dustin as a child had somehow come back to life to terrorize him again. He'd gotten away, and it was leaving him alone now. It was either live life as he always had, or spend the rest of his days eating tapioca pudding with a plastic spoon in the loony bin. Personally, Dustin wasn't a big fan of pudding.

Mother and son had not discussed the events of his abduction since the day it happened. She did not know the true identity of who he had been with, nor did she seem to care. There was an unspoken routine that developed every night before bed where Dustin would go and check all the locks on the doors and windows, with her re-checking after he was done, just to make sure. Beyond that, both were silent on the matter.

Sometimes, he had problems going to sleep at night. He was convinced it had heard Desta that day when she'd threatened it and was taking heed to her warning, but where *was* it; what was it *doing*? Had it crawled back into the ground, pulling dirt onto itself until it was comfortable enough to rest again?

Dustin had ardently avoided Hillcrest Cemetery ever since that day. He wouldn't drive or walk past it, and he wouldn't watch the news. Once, he'd been scrolling through Facebook and came across a post regarding break-ins at local liquor stores in the area. It was believed the same perpetrator had committed the crimes. While no fingerprints were found at the scenes, there was one commonality that linked all the occurrences together: muddy boot prints, believed to be from a size 9 or 10 sole. Trevor had worn a 9 and a half. Dustin blocked the page.

He hadn't heard anything about local grave robbers or graves that had been dug up in the recent weeks, and he was sure Desta would have been notified if such a thing had happened at Trevor's plot. Either he had filled the hole back in really well, or no one had been there to notice. Dustin suspected it was a combination of the two. He hadn't visited Trevor's grave in well over three years. It was set far back in the cemetery, near the World War 2 vets. One would not even know it was there unless they were specifically looking for it, which most people weren't. Trevor, Mark Geist, and John

Brennegan were persona non grata as far as the people of Berthshire were concerned.

Every now and then, he'd find something left behind by the presence that had stayed with them. Desta had sent him down to clean the basement a couple of weeks back. The landlord was coming to fix a leaky pipe, and she wanted everything in tip-top shape for when he arrived.

While he was cleaning, Dustin had went behind the new washer and dryer to sweep up dust bunnies. There, he discovered two empty bottles of St. Ives on the ground, along with discarded cigarette butts and a turkey leg that had been stripped clean down to the bone. Apparently, Trevor had celebrated Thanksgiving after all. Needless to say, he stopped venturing down to the basement after that.

The nightmares lessened, but didn't stop completely. Dustin would dream of an endless cornfield enveloped in blood-red. He would be running, the sound of a large tractor growing closer and closer. Eventually, he would turn around and see it right behind him: the John Deere from Cindy's house. It was washed and painted like it was brand new. The shiny blades stood twenty feet off the ground, rotating around each other like the red stripes in a barber's pole. And sitting in the driver's seat, pulling the levers and directing the show, the desiccated corpse of Trevor Taylor.

"Come-come-come on, little bro, we're farmers now!" It was always dressed the same, wearing blue jean overalls and a large straw hat. It would smile at him with broken green teeth and press a button that sent the whirling blades into a frantic overdrive.

"COME WITH ME TO HELL-HELL-HELL-HELLY-HELL, BUDDY! THEY GOT THE GOOD SHIT!"

The tractor would move at an impossibly fast pace as Dustin tried to run from it. The mechanical whirring of the blades would reach a deafening crescendo as he felt it bearing down on him. Then he would jolt awake. Sometimes, Desta would be sitting beside him, wiping the sweat off his forehead with a towel and holding his hand.

"You were screaming," she would say. "You all right?" He would affirm that he was even though he wasn't, and she would go back to bed. He'd wait until she was gone and then turn on every light in the room.

Sometimes, he would stand by the window at night, leaning on the air conditioner, looking outside. He knew he wouldn't be able to see anything, but he looked, anyway, wondering what was out there, hiding amongst the crickets. Watching, waiting.

The relationship between Dustin and Desta had subtly shifted, as well. They'd still joke and banter with each other, but the conversations would end awkwardly rather than amicably, as if both knew something had been changed between them but that they needed to maintain some sort of facade that it hadn't. Once, Desta had asked Dustin some odd questions that made him feel uncomfortable.

"Hey," she said while they were watching TV in the living room together. She was on the recliner, and he was on the couch.

"Yeah, what's up?'

Desta grabbed the remote. Ken Jennings was in the middle of asking a question on *Jeopardy*.

"What plant is known to 'eat' the insects that happen to find themselves trapped inside its cavernous maw?"

One of the contestants was beginning to answer "What is a--" when Desta muted the show.

"You would tell me if you were in trouble and needed me, right? Like if maybe you were in a bad situation and needed me to help you get out of it? Maybe someone from school, or a friend, or maybe even a girl, anything like that?"

"Uh, yeah," he said. "I guess. You mean like if I pissed

someone off, was gonna get in a fight, something like that, Mom?"

"No," she said, unconsciously patting the pack of cigarettes in her pants pocket. She had started again after the day at Cindy's. So much for not tempting the unbeliever. "I mean really bad. Like if maybe you tried something and really liked it, then it happened more, and you couldn't stop, and the other person wouldn't let you stop. Something like that."

"You mean like drugs. Like what Trevor was into when he was my age." No need to sugarcoat it. He knew exactly what she was getting at, though asking if there was a girl involved seemed kind of odd.

"Yes," she said, wishing she had a cigarette between her lips right at that precise moment. "Something like that. It's okay to tell me. I won't be mad."

"No," he said. "I've tried weed a couple times, but never bought it from anyone. And I've drank a little, but that's it."

"Okay," Desta said, satisfied. "I'm going to ask you another question, and I need your full honesty with this."

"Okay," Dustin said hesitantly, not knowing what she was about to throw at him.

"When you met Cindy a couple weeks ago, my friend with the ranch, was there anything that maybe you want to tell me?"

"I…" Dustin didn't know what to say. He was dumbfounded. "You mean like what happened when I went lights out on you, if I remember anything from that?"

"No…I mean, yes. Or anything else."

"Mom, I don't know what you're talking about."

Desta let out an exasperated sigh and smiled at him.

"Of course you don't, and that's a good thing. I'm going to step outside and get some air. Here's the remote." She handed it to him as she walked past the couch to the foyer to get her shoes. He watched her closely as she went out, wondering if maybe she'd been drinking, or anything else. The entire conversation was so bizarre and off-putting.

Dustin knew she was smoking again, but decided to stay silent on the matter. While he'd still mess with her and pick on her for other things, he possessed a newfound reverence for her that left certain topics off-limits. Due to her protective nature regarding the matter, he assumed smoking to be one of the things he needed to just leave alone. He decided to do the same thing in regards to her strange inquiries. Again, more questions that he didn't want to know the answers to.

The only person he told about the events surrounding Thanksgiving was his buddy, Steve, and only then did he give out the same surface-level details as he'd given his mother: a junkie had repeatedly broken into the house and forced him to steal Mom's car, Dustin had driven to the river and fought him off, and the guy hadn't been back since. Steve didn't need to know any more than that.

"You were in a fight and *won*?" Steve asked as Dustin had recounted the story over lunch. "Bro, I gotta see the dude who lost to you. Probably a total bitchasaurus rex."

Say that to his face, Dustin thought as Steve stuffed his mouth with nachos and salsa. *Or what's left of it.*

The horror of what he'd faced that day in the cornfield and in the car later that night didn't completely leave Dustin —how could it? His brother was still very likely out there somewhere, undead, hungry, seething with insane rage after being thwarted and then ultimately exiled from the only place it knew. But it was leaving him alone, at least for the time being, and Dustin was thankful for that.

But still, he wondered. What had its plans been for him? Why had it listened to Desta and stayed away? For these questions, he didn't have answers, and hopefully never would. What Dustin did know was that he would probably keep an eye on his surroundings until his dying day, ready for it to come back when the rage grew to be too much and it sought its vengeance.

Unfortunately, sometimes when we are overly vigilant, we miss the danger standing right in front of us, watching in broad daylight. Dustin made this mistake, and every horrible thing that followed was the direct result of it.

CHAPTER 14

Christmas was right around the corner, and Desta was just about sick of it. She couldn't walk into Walmart without almost being trampled just to get a can of green beans for dinner. Everyone always seemed to be in a rush, despite the fact that there was still a week and a half before the holiday. This was not to mention the Salvation Army Santas, standing outside the store doors, guilt-tripping people into dropping their hard-earned cash into the identical red tins hanging from rusty red chains in front of *both* entryways. While she loved this time of the year, these were things she could do without for roughly the next eternity.

She had just gotten home from Target. A cold front had swept through the region the week before, and the roads were starting to get slick at night. Twice, she'd almost fishtailed while coming down Bonniebrook Lane in Braxton. Two big drop-offs were on either side of the road, each of them going down about five hundred feet or so. Thank God there had been no one else on the road with her at the time, or things may have turned out very differently. All to get Dustin the brand new PlayStation 4 before it sold out. Simply put, she was not in the mood to mess around that evening.

Unlucky for Dustin, as when Desta entered the house, she was greeted with him shouting at someone how they were a "bloody tampon-eating whore monger." Wordlessly, she walked right past him to the TV. She reached around to the outlet behind the entertainment center and pulled out every plug until the green ring on the front of the X-Box went dark.

"Yo!" Dustin yelled in surprise. "I was in the middle of an eighteen-person kill streak! What in the actual balls!?"

"Not dealing with it tonight, Dustin," Desta said as she made her way to the kitchen. "Keep it up, and the next things to go are the headset and microphone. Don't push me."

"This is complete bullshit," Dustin muttered. "I'm almost an adult."

"What was that?"

"I said you're beautiful, and I'm grateful you are doing your part not to let me wander down the path of a misguided deviant."

Desta poked her head out through the doorway.

"Isn't it funny, how sarcasm and the truth can be the exact same thing?"

He raised his hand to his lips and blew her a kiss.

"Get your number after dinner, sweet thang?"

Desta reached into her pocket and pulled out a long ribbon of paper.

"The only numbers we're going to go over are the ones on the receipts for all your Christmas shit. You're driving me to a homeless shelter."

"Oh yeah? At least we'll have a bunch of super bad ass stuff to keep us entertained while we're there." He flashed a cheesy grin at her. She turned and went back into the kitchen.

"Hey, buddy!" she called out. "If you think for one second you'll be coming with me, you're going to be sorely disappointed. I'll leave you outside, with…the…"

Dustin waited a few seconds for her to finish. Nothing.

"Leave me outside with the what, Mom? What were you going to say, Oompa Loompa in an apron?"

Silence.

"Mom? Hey, Mom! You still there?" He got off the couch. It wasn't like her to get distracted so easily. He went through the doorway into the kitchen.

"Mom? Everything okay? Hey, Mom?"

She was standing with her back to him, facing the back door leading outside.

"Hey, sorry about the Oompa Loompa crack. You're at least hobbit status. Hey! Yo!"

Desta started, turning around quickly. In one hand, she was holding a black plastic ladle. In the other was her largest kitchen knife.

"Huh, what? Sorry, I was talking, then I thought I saw a bear going through the trash outside. Sorry, false alarm."

She hurried back to the stove. The chicken noodle soup she'd been cooking had boiled over a little bit. Thick lines of creamy yellow broth were dripping down the sides of the pot. She grabbed a cleaning rag from the drawer Dustin was forbidden to touch and wiped it off.

"A *bear*?" Dustin asked, intrigued. "What kind of bear? A black bear? Brown bear? Black bears are pretty tame."

"Uh-huh," Desta said as she put the dial to the burner on low and stirred the soup. "I don't know what it was. Not a bear."

"So, what was it?"

"What was what, hon?" Ever since his abduction, Desta had gotten back into the habit of calling Dustin pet names without even realizing it.

"You said you thought you saw a bear, but it wasn't. So, what did you think it was? You were holding a knife, but you're not making anything that needs cut. Must've freaked you out."

"Oh!" Desta exclaimed with a laugh. "No, it was just a big

raccoon or something. Maybe a groundhog. I was tapping on the window to scare it away. I heard the can get tipped over and thought it was something a lot bigger. No worries." She went back to stirring.

Dustin approached the door and looked out. It was night-time now, despite only being 5:30 PM—a lovely benefit of living in the northern hemisphere during both winter *and* daylight saving time. The light from the back porch allowed him to see the large black garbage can, lying on its side on the sidewalk. The white bag he'd taken out earlier was hanging halfway out, its contents scattered all over the ground around it. Thin slash marks were apparent throughout the bag, culminating in one large tear near the top. Mom was right: probably a raccoon, or maybe a bobcat.

"I'm gonna go out to check," he said, reaching for the lock. "Maybe I can get a picture for Instagram."

"*DON'T!*" Desta yelled as he was turning the lock.

"What? But wh—"

"Do you forget what happened to you a few weeks ago? And now you want to just go traipsing around in the dark? And for what, an *Instagram* picture? You almost died, you big dumb ass. Use your head."

Dustin thought about what she just said and let go of the lock. As much as he didn't want to admit it, Mom was right, righter than she even knew. Trevor had been watching him and preparing what it did for who knew how long. Would it not stand to reason that it'd have even *more* patience and resolve after Dustin had bested it? Trevor could easily dominate him when he was a small child. It hadn't been such a simple task now that Dustin was fully grown. If it was going to attack again, it would want to plan better this time, catch him off guard and get him when he was least expecting it.

Like knocking over the garbage can and ripping holes in the bag to lure you both outside, pick you and Mom off, one by one. Get revenge guerrilla style.

"You're right," Dustin said. "Better to be safe than sorry."

"That's right," Desta said while taking a small spoon and scooping a little soup out of the pot. "Now, come try this. I might have put too much salt in it."

She held the spoon up, her other hand underneath it to catch any spillage. Dustin came over. She lifted it and tipped it into his mouth.

"Too much salt?" Dustin said after swallowing. "Are you crazy? It tastes perfect, Mom. Better than usual, actually."

She blushed.

"I tried a new recipe where I add in a little bit of beef stock and garlic powder. I was scared how it was going to turn out. I've gotten a little rusty since I've been managing the diner and not cooking there anymore."

"Well, you still 'got the knack,' as the kids say. Seriously, it's really good, Mom."

Desta was about to respond when Dustin's phone went off in his front pocket. He pulled it out and pressed on the screen. A slight smile creased his lips.

"Ohhhh," Desta said, batting her eyelashes at him. "Is that Staaaaaaaacy?"

"Yes, oh one who harbored me in her womb. It's Stacy." Despite his jovial tone, Dustin was blushing. They'd been texting back and forth ever since he asked her to the Winter Ball, and Desta made sure to make a show of it every chance she got. While it was funny at times, it did irritate him a little.

"What's she up to? She better not be sending you any nudies." She pointed the spoon at him threateningly.

"*MOM*! Dude, what the fuck?" Dustin said this as his fingers sped typed a response back. "You know I don't do that type of stuff. Besides, we're just friends."

"Well," Desta said matter-of-factly, "you should invite your friend over for dinner. This completely innocent friend whom you hold no romantic affinity towards."

Dustin's phone dinged again. He restrained himself from checking it. It would just give Mom more fodder.

"Uh-uh," Dustin said emphatically. "All you would do is tell her stories about wiping my butt when I was a baby and try to scare her away. No thanks."

"No," Desta said while getting her own spoon of soup to try. "I'd tell her about when I did that *after* you were a baby." She sucked the soup down. "You're right—that *is* really good."

Dustin shook his head and made his way to the living room. His stomach was rumbling. He was ready to eat.

"Hey! What time's dinner, anyway?"

"Seven o'clock!" Desta called out. "Plenty of time for your new girlfriend to put her make-up on and come over!"

"Eat a fat one, Mom! Respectfully!"

Seeing she was done with the back and forth for now, Dustin plopped on the couch and finally satisfied his impulses by reading what Stacy had sent to him. They'd been discussing potential colleges they might apply to. Pretty mundane stuff, but he was quickly discovering that Stacy could make the mundane seem quite enthralling, at least to him.

I was also thinking of applying to Penn State, but I doubt I'd get in, her message said.

Aw Im sure you could Ur so smart, read Dustin's reply.

He looked at the bottom right corner of the screen. Delivered, not Read yet.

Having a moment to think, Dustin remembered the incident in the kitchen when Mom wasn't answering him and was holding the butcher knife. *Holding* wasn't quite the right word for it; she'd been *clutching* it in her right hand. The blade had been facing forward at an angle, as if she was in preparation to ward something off with it, or, even worse, defend herself. Had she thought the same as him, that maybe the fiend had returned for a second go at them both?

I already died once, you can't die twice

What a shock it would be for Mom to stand face to half-a-face with Trevor again after all these years. How much more of a shock it would be if she had to use the knife, only to discover it had no impact whatsoever. Could a dead thing even bleed? Dustin's counter-attack on it had caused some form of pain, that much was at least established. It could be hurt, at least for a short period of time. If he ever saw it again, he'd use this knowledge to his advantage.

DING!

Dustin smiled to himself a little bit and grabbed his phone. As he did, he reminded himself not to become too complacent. There was a walking horror show out there that knew all of his fears and weaknesses. It was so easy to forget the worst of things with the passage of time. It wasn't a mistake he could afford to make again.

"Dustin, I'm leaving!" called Desta from the foyer.

Putting his phone down for the first time in an hour, Dustin got out of bed and poked his head out of his room.

"What do you mean you're leaving? We haven't even had dinner yet! What do you have, a hot date or something?"

"Actually," Desta said as she made her way back through the hallway, adjusting her earring, "yes, I do. Cindy knows someone who just moved down this way from her church. She got us talking online, and he asked me out for coffee. So yes, if that's your idea of a 'hot date,' I have one." She began fumbling with the other earring.

"Well, if you're going out dressed like *that*, I'd think you were going out for more than just coffee."

Desta was dressed in her favorite white button-up blouse and the black skirt that she only saved for special occasions. It wasn't form-fitting and went down below her knee caps, but still, she didn't wear *these* clothes unless she was having a meeting of significant importance.

"Wait till you see my footwear," Desta said, winking at him.

Dustin's mouth dropped to an exaggerated O. He let out a gasp.

"No. Not…*the high heels!*"

She nodded with a grave look on her face.

"Yes, the oh-so-dreaded high heels. The black ones, to be more specific."

Coming out now, Dustin made a tsk-tsk sound as he followed Desta to her room.

"Well, looks like I better start cleaning out the storage room and get the crib out. We're about to have a new baby up in here."

The sound of water running in Desta's sink came on for a couple of seconds and then back off. She emerged, her auburn hair done up in a ponytail. Dustin's stomach cramped a little bit as he noted that she was wearing lipstick, the dark plum one, to be more specific. This really was a big deal to her. He looked her over once and then forced his eyes away. Mother or not, Desta was a good-looking woman when she felt the urge to flaunt it.

"The only crying you'll hear around here is your own after I shove one of these high heels down your throat. Now, come zip me up before you get a preview of that."

Desta turned and lifted her hair from her shoulders. Dustin approached, putting one hand on her back while using the other for the zipper of the blouse. She felt so delicate; he could feel her breathing against the fabric as he steadied himself. He zipped her up and let go immediately. For some reason, he was thinking of Stacy. Also…something else, from a long time ago. Flowers. Maybe roses.

"Thank you," Desta said, walking around him towards the foyer again.

"Hey, uh," Dustin said as he followed her. "What if, you know, something happens, like a fire, or an emergency, or…"

She looked up at him while she was strapping her first heel on. An expression of loving sympathy washed over her face. In this state, Desta didn't look just pretty; she looked absolutely stunning.

Flowers…knife…Trevor…a man.

"If *he* comes back? Like how I was scared in the kitchen earlier?" There was no need for Desta to spell out who *he* was. They both knew who she was referring to.

"Yeah. Yeah, I guess so." Dustin began rubbing his neck. "I've just been a little freaked out, especially at night. I guess we've both been."

"Yeah," Desta agreed. She had not yet begun putting the other shoe on. "Honey, I can stay home if you want me to. There's always another night. I kind of don't want to go, anyway. Anything you need, I'm here."

"Well, I think—"

DING!

Dustin pulled out his phone and read the message on the screen.

"You know what, Mom, go ahead and go out. Stacy's gonna Facetime me and help me with English homework. You know how much I need that."

"Oh, okay," Desta said, sounding dejected. She began slipping on the other heel. "You just make sure to lock *everything* when I step out that door. And don't—"

"Answer for anyone or go outside by myself," he finished for her. "I know the routine, Mom. Go, have fun. I'll be okay."

Desta felt an ache in her heart. A few weeks ago, he'd needed her more than he had in over a decade. Now, some girl was in the picture, and he was suddenly a man—independent, able to fend for himself, wanting for nothing. Next year, he would go to college and leave her here all by herself. He really was growing up. Part of her resented him for it.

"Okay," she said. "I will have a good time. A great time. Going now." She looked behind her. He was on the couch, phone inches from his face as he typed away. The resentment turned into a deep sadness. She was losing him to the world, and maybe that was necessary, but it still didn't take away the increasing hollowness growing inside of her. Oh well, this is what had to happen. Desta just had to accept this inevitable fact of life and do what she needed to do to deal with it.

"Bye, sweetie, see you later!"

No answer. Desta felt that sadness knife through her again and closed the door.

CHAPTER 15

"So, an adverb would be used for..." Dustin had a pen in his hand and an open notebook on his lap. The page he had opened was covered in various notes and markings.

"Think of it like an adjective that's describing how something is done. A descriptor of an action. Ad-verb." Stacy's face filled the iPhone screen. The only time Dustin took his eyes away was when he had to write something in his notepad.

"Okay," he said while jotting down what she had just said. "Give me an example."

"So," Stacy said, "think of the word sad. 'He was sad about beginning his day.' Now, the adverb version would be sadly. 'He woke up and began his day sadly.' It's describing *how* his day is starting rather than *what* he is doing to start his day."

He stopped writing.

"Hold up, wait a minute. How is starting off your day 'sad' an action? Do you wake up and just make an active decision to start crying when you go down to make cereal? I don't get it."

She giggled. "In the context of how sentence structure

works, yes. The question you should ask yourself is, how does one start off their day 'sadly'? Or how does one look at you happily, or angrily? 'I am angry' is a pretty straightforward statement. How does angrily look? What is it actually describing?"

"Uhhh…" Dustin said, his eyes squinted and glazed over. "You lost me at sentence structure."

"Okay," Stacy said. "Here's what you need to know for the test: most of the time, if it ends in 'ly,' it's an adverb. If it doesn't and it's an action, it's a verb."

"So, what's a pronoun? Like a noun with a capital at the beginning?"

Stacy took her glasses off and massaged the bridge of her nose. Dustin thought she looked really pretty with her glasses off.

"We'll deal with that next time. Just remember, "ly" for adverbs. Merrily, suspiciously, halfheartedly. And try not to use them a lot. Stephen King says they are lazy fillers that don't actually describe what is being attempted to be described. Use them sparingly."

"Ha! You just used one!"

"Used one what?"

"An adverb! 'Sparingly.' It ends with ly. Spare, sparingly"

She rubbed her nose again.

"Dustin…just, let's keep it simple for right now. Don't call it an adverb unless I tell you it's an adverb. And yes, you're right. Sparingly is indeed an adverb, so good job."

He raised an eyebrow.

"Oh, really? So just do what the boss lady says?"

He had to restrain himself from knocking his own shin into the table after the words came out of his mouth. *Boss lady.* Had he ever even attempted to flirt with a girl before? (He put his attention back on her before his mind attempted to answer that question.)

"That's right," Stacy said, restraining herself from giggling again. "What I say goes until further notice."

A surge of relief flowed through him. She took the lame joke as he wanted her to take it. Maybe she thought it was just as stupid as he did—that part didn't matter. She didn't reject the comment or go quiet. That was a very good sign.

He threw her a military salute from his forehead to the air.

"Yes, ma'am. Roger that, 10-4."

"Ohhh, God," she said, laughing now. "Well, listen, Maverick, I have a thing with my mom. She's going to teach me how to make homemade lasagna, but I can still text you in between. Is that okay?"

All the excitement rushed out of him like air leaving a punctured balloon, but he said nothing. They'd been on the phone for over an hour, and he was feeling a little drained. He got like this sometimes, especially whenever he indulged in too much of a good thing. This would be the perfect time to stop the conversation, while they were both still in good spirits.

"Yeah, that's totally fine," Dustin said. "Actually, I might play some video games to unwind a little bit, so I might not respond right away."

Who was he fooling? He practically lived to hear his phone go off now. He would even pause Call of Duty to respond to her sometimes. *That* was a big deal.

"Okay," Stacy said. "Text me when you're done. No big deal."

"No, no, no!" he said quickly. "You can text me while I'm playing. It's okay."

Unlike Dustin, Stacy was perfectly content with going for long periods of time without talking. He knew this was normal and something he didn't make a big deal about, but he absolutely hated contacting her first. His initiating the conversation made him feel like an annoyance, while her starting it made him feel wanted and like he was safe to say what he really felt without worry of it being overwhelming for her.

"Okay, I will," Stacy said. "Chat you in a little bit?"

"I'll be here, ready and waiting." Ohhh, how he wanted to slap himself.

Just talk fucking normal, dude. She doesn't need all this weird, flirty bullshit.

"All righty. Talk to you soon, Maverick."

"Over and out, Goose."

Stacy's hand blacked out the screen, and then the call ended. Dustin let out a sigh and put his phone on the coffee table. He hated that she almost always ended the conversations. It made him feel desperate. Sometimes, he would tell her he had things to do just so it came across like he had a life outside of her. He wondered if she was just as disappointed when they stopped talking as he was. He doubted it. Even Mom got fed up with him and needed a break sometimes, and that was saying a lot.

Risking overthinking it, he grabbed the new X-Box controller he bought two weeks ago and switched the console on. He waited for it to load and immediately went to the settings screen to check his username. DustyRoads187, just as it should have been. This was another new habit he'd added to his routine ever since Trevor had made his visit from the great beyond.

He loaded up Call of Duty and got to shooting. Every now and then, he'd stop for a second and hit the side button on the phone to see if he had any new messages. Of course, he didn't; his notification tone would have gone off if he did. But compulsion forced him to check, anyway.

Dustin played for a while before looking up to the clock. 8:53. It had been nearly forty-five minutes ago that he'd gotten off the phone with Stacy.

It's okay, he thought. *She's just making lasagna with her mom. She's still going with you to the dance, and she still likes you. Just chill.*

Or, an intrusive voice said, *she just got off the phone with you to talk to the guy she's really interested in. She's sending pics of herself and flirting with him back, and actually laughing at his jokes instead of just pretending like she does with you. She's just using you for attention when someone better isn't around, and that makes you the joke, doesn't it? Who knows, little bro, maybe I even have a shot. I'll tear that pussy up!*

"Shut up," Dustin said out loud. "She's not like that, and you know it. She's cooking with her mom, and that's okay. Nothing to worry about."

Yeah-yeah-yeah-yeah there is! How many guys you think she's blown? Think of that—all those times that pretty little mouth has went to work. But not for you. Never for you. Mr. Mommy Man. She's never gonna talk to your bitch ass agai—

DING!

The sound of the phone instantly silenced Trevor's dead voice. Dustin restrained himself for all of thirty seconds before he had the screen open and was reading the text.

Be home in 45 minutes. Not a good match. Leave some soup out for me. Love you.

FUCK, MOM! his inner-voice shouted. It was bad enough, having to sit here and obsess like a crazy person, but then to get his hopes up just for it to be nothing…that annoyed him to no end.

He took a few minutes to let his irritation level go down before texting her back.

Ok b safe Luv you to

Checking the top of the screen one last time to make sure he didn't have any missed messages, Dustin set the phone down and started a new game in Call of Duty. This sort of thinking was something he needed to get a hold on, and now. Just because he was lonely didn't mean he could depend on someone he was attracted to to keep him some form of company every waking moment. He had other things, other people he could talk to, other things he could be doing. He needed to focus on those, as well.

Like Mom…a hybrid of his and Trevor's voice said inside of him. *She's the one person you can trust and say anything to. What if Trevor wasn't back for you at all? What if it was for her? What if that still is the reason? She looked so pretty tonight, in her nice white blouse.*

"Stop it."

The screen on the TV exploded in a cloud of white. He'd been killed in the game with a frag. Wait for the respawn.

He's still out there, watching from the bushes and the trees, waiting to get her. Put his hands all over her.

A bloody ring showed now. Shot in the head. Respawn.

Wrap his arms around her from behind, feel her panting in her chest. That silky black skirt, rubbing against his knee.

Stabbed in the face. Respawn.

He'd have control over her. Trevor would be the boss man. *He'd run his gnarled, flaking hands down her front…*

Dead. Respsawn.

Slide them down her thighs to her knees.

Blood everywhere. Red roses. Respawn.

Push up her skirt.

A screaming man, and then a child. Mom in the bathroom.

"Go back to bed, baby."

Move his hand between her thighs.

DING!

Game Over. No more respawns.

Dustin snapped out of it and looked at his phone.

Hey, you still playing video games?

Not wanting to seem too eager, Dustin gave it a few minutes before replying.

Not anymore Having a rough nite

He hit send. After thinking for a second: *How did cooking with ur mom go?*

He hated sending one message after the other without waiting for a response first, but he felt the need to do this now for two reasons: one, he didn't want to make the conversation all about him; two, he didn't want to explain out in detail why he was having a rough night. After the absolutely revolting litany of thoughts he'd just had, he would have to lie to Stacy, and that was something he wanted to avoid doing at all costs.

His phone went off again. He prayed to the void above that she had just answered his question and didn't ask any of her own regarding his first message. He read the reply and felt immediate relief.

It went really well. Mom's noodles were cut a lot better than mine, but it's okay. Just need to practice. Thank you for asking.

Dustin was typing whenever the phone buzzed in his hand again.

A rough night? Oh no, what happened? The boss lady demands to know. She followed the text with a yellow emoji with wide eyes and an open mouth.

Thinking, he finished his first message, telling her she was welcome and that she was right; she just had to practice some more, and then she'd have the best lasagna ever. Immediately, the message status went from Delivered to Read. Dustin waited a little while to see if the three dots popped up in the bottom of the chat to indicate she was typing something. Maybe they could focus on her ventures with pasta, and she would forget he mentioned anything about himself. He tested to see if she was still waiting by sending a smiley face. Again, it went from Delivered to Read, no typing dots following it. He'd talked to her enough to know she was waiting for him to answer her question.

And Im just stuck in my mind tonight To much thinking Nothin bad happened, promise

Read. *Now,* she was typing. He looked away for ten seconds, then looked again. Still typing. Ten more seconds, *still* typing. Finally, after three ten-second intervals, his phone dinged.

Yeah, doing anything with pasta sucks. Mom gets super frustrated. And hey, if you need to talk about what you're thinking, I'm here. I know what it's like to sit around, stuck in your own head. Really, you can tell me anything.

Dustin thought of what his response would look like if he were to truly take her up on that offer.

Oh, sure, Stacy. Well, my dead brother's corpse camped in my house for who knows how long, then took me to the river by his old meth dealer's house to drown me. He had me snorting coke at ten years old and would beat the shit out of me if I didn't. Now, he looks like something out of a Clive Barker movie. Oh, by the way, I was having violent, incestuous thoughts about my mother right before you texted me. Now, what time was it that you wanted me to pick you up for the dance and meet your parents again?

I am ok Just thots from the past but thank you 4 asking is what he sent instead.

His phone dinged again a few seconds later.

Okay…but I do want you to know that. I am here. Seriously, Dustin. But hey, I'm going to go to bed now. I'm soooo tired. I think I might be coming down with a cold. See you in the gym in the morning, okay?

He told her good night. She replied with the same words, a snoring emoji accompanying them. Then the little green dot beside her name went away. She was gone for the evening.

Desta came in through the door around fifteen minutes later. Her cheeks were slightly red, and her hair was undone and down to her shoulders. There was just the slightest hint of a stumble in her gait.

"Hey, sweetie," she said while undoing her shoes. "How was your night? You just play video games and talk to what's-her-name?"

"Stacy," Dustin said, knowing full well Mom knew her name. "And yeah. We studied, then I played a few rounds with Steve and Tay. Nothing too exciting. I guess you and church guy didn't hit it off so good?"

Desta kicked her shoes off and walked into the living room. Diverting from her usual route to the recliner, she instead sat down beside Dustin on the sofa. He inched himself away from her a little, the intrusive thoughts from earlier still fresh in his mind.

"Nope, all wrong. I thought Cindy was bad with the Bible thumping stuff, but holy shit, literally. All the guy tried to do was convert me the whole time. I probably know more about Jesus than he does at this point. I was definitely praying to Him to get me out of there, that's for sure." Not thinking, Desta took a cigarette from her purse and lit it right while she was sitting beside Dustin. She was already four drags in before she turned and saw the surprised revulsion etched on his face.

"*Shit*, sorry, baby. I stopped and had a few drinks at the Moose before I came back. Not thinking." She pulled a portable ashtray from her purse. "Is it okay? It's only one. I'll spray Febreeze after."

"No," Dustin said, "it's okay." It really wasn't, but he wasn't about to start an argument with her. He thought of the cigarette butts he'd found in the basement behind the washer. It's not like it was the first time there had been smoking inside the house. At least the offender was actually *alive* this time.

"I really am lucky with you," Desta said, blowing smoke away from him. "A lot of kids in your situation would be into a lot of bad stuff right now."

"Situation?" Dustin asked, stifling a cough. The acrid smell from the cigarette was stinging the inside of his throat and nostrils. His eyes were watering, and his nose was beginning to run. Desta didn't seem to notice.

"Living with a single mom, dad dying, brother dying. Some of the things you've been through. And now you're getting ready to go to college, and you have a little girlfriend. I'm really proud of you."

She ashed into the tray. It was actually more like a cup with a hole on top to keep the contents from spilling out. Dustin wondered how long she had actually been smoking again.

"She's not my girlfriend," he said with a sniffle. "We're good friends. I asked her to the dance because neither of us had anyone to go with."

Desta laughed. In her current inebriated state, it came out more as a cackle. She took a big hit from the Marlboro.

"Come on, sweetie, who are you trying to fool? She's all I ever hear you talking about to your X-Box friends, and you're practically glued to your phone. You really like her."

"Yeah," he said. "I guess I do."

He stared at the Call of Duty start screen while Desta finished her cigarette. The entire top half of the living room looked like there was a noxious cloud of smog hanging below it. Feeling the tickle in the back of his throat starting to become too bothersome, Dustin grabbed his phone and stood up, announcing he was going to lie down for the evening.

"Okay, sweetie," Desta said, also standing up. "I'm going to get some soup and go back. Send your wonderful Aunt Cindy a text, thanking her for trying to hook me up with St. Peter with an accounting degree. That was the only other thing he talked about besides sin, and how I needed to repent before it was too late. Riveting stuff."

He didn't like this, how Mom was talking to him about her failed date like he was her adult equal. On the rare occasions she did go out, she'd come back home and share only the most minimal of details with him. "It was fun. We danced.

Okay, get back to bed so you can be ready for school in the morning," that kind of stuff. Her giving a play-by-play of the evening with her own matured commentary left him feeling disconcerted, like she was telling him secret things he shouldn't be hearing.

"Gotchya," he said, starting back to his room." There's always more fish in the ocean. You'll snag one, eventually."

"Was everything okay here?" she asked quickly, not wanting to end the conversation yet. "I was worried about you all night. I shouldn't have left you alone. I'm sorry."

"Nope, no incidents to report," he said as he inched his way back towards the hall. "I believe our past guest is one hundred percent gone, probably hobo-ing his way to Sandusky on a train, a ticket in his hand and a pocket full of dreams."

Desta let out a throaty laugh and snagged another cigarette from her purse. She made her way towards the kitchen.

"I'll smoke this one outside. I plan on quitting again after this week, just so you know.

He nodded. "I know you will. Have a good night, Mom."

"I love you," she called back. He cringed at hearing the words. He never offered them to anyone out loud and very rarely ever had them directed his way, especially from her. She was acting so *weird* lately.

"Love you, too," he said.

Dustin made his way back and got ready for bed. Before switching on his nightly YouTube video, he went into his phone settings and turned all ringers to silent. He looked at Facebook Messenger one last time. It said Stacy had been offline for over an hour. He felt a surge of reassurance.

You have to stop doing this, dude. It's going to eventually drive you both crazy, like Trevor did with you, and maybe himself. People need their space, and you need yours. Don't forget that.

He turned the latest L.A. Beast video on and lay down. He

didn't like thinking of Trevor before bed. More so, he didn't like making *comparisons* of himself to Trevor before bed, or to consider the possibility that maybe they were more alike than Dustin wished to believe. That in itself was scarier than any monster waiting outside of his door in the middle of the night.

CHAPTER 16

Yawning, Dustin reached over and hit the off button on his alarm clock. It was such common practice to him at this point that he didn't even have to look anymore to know where it was. Biggest button, third one in from the left. Never failed.

As per routine, he got out of bed and got his clothes together. Then, he went into the bathroom to brush his teeth and take a shower. When that was done, he went back to his room to get his school stuff ready. It was 6:50 AM. The sun was already starting to show outside. He was still half awake, trying to get oriented. It took him a couple of minutes to retrieve his phone from the pile of sheets and blankets on the bed. He disconnected it from the charger and clicked it on, searching for the now familiar circular icon in the upper-left-hand corner. There it was. That message could only be from one person. Fully awake now, Dustin opened the app. His heart almost dropped upon seeing her words.

Good morning, handsome, followed by a yawning emoji. The time sent was 6:38 AM.

Dustin immediately began typing a response. *Good*

morning is what it started out as, which was simple enough. The complicated part came when figuring out how to end it. Beautiful, pretty lady, gorgeous? Definitely not gorgeous— Dustin didn't know how to spell it, and he didn't want to take a chance with auto-correct making him look like an idiot. He fumbled around with the keyboard for a while before finally deciding on something safe that would still get the point across.

Good morning boss lady I hope u got some beauty sleep (not that u need it)

Dustin hit send, then pocketed the phone, not even bothering to turn the notification alerts back on. His day had already begun the best way it possibly could; he wanted to bask in what she said for a while before reading any further responses. She'd be there waiting for him when he got back.

He went out to make himself a bowl of cereal. When that was finished, he went across the street to wait for the bus (after triple-checking all the locks in the house, of course). Desta had already left for work. While the diner didn't open until 8:00 AM, she needed to be there to make sure the fryers were on, the veggies pre-chopped, and that the balance in the register matched what it had been the night before. She was usually gone a good thirty to forty-five minutes before Dustin even woke up.

As he was waiting, he decided to check his phone. No new messages. That was odd, but not unprecedented. Sometimes, Stacy had minor chores to do, like letting their dog out or cleaning the breakfast dishes before leaving for school. She lived close enough to the senior high that she would walk as long as the weather permitted, so sometimes her morning duties prevented them from talking until they both saw each other in the gym.

Bored, he scrolled through their chat box and looked through their conversation from last night leading into today.

Just a couple of simple sentences, but the implications were enough to get the butterflies in his stomach fluttering. He looked down at the last message he sent to see the status.

Read 10 minutes ago.

That *was* weird. Usually, Stacy would reply almost immediately if she saw what he sent her. He looked up to the status bar beside her name. The green dot was visible. Online. Now, the icy fingers of worry were slowly tapping their way up his vertebrae.

Dude, you've only been talking for three weeks. You just flirted with each other for the first time less than a half an hour ago. She's probably taking it all in, just like you are. Everything is fine, and you'll see each other in twenty minutes. It's cool, man.

The bus came rolling up the street a few minutes later. It had just started flurrying outside, so for once, Dustin was actually happy to climb aboard. He checked his messages all the way to school. Status: Read, no little typing dots. Stacy was online the entire time. Dustin decided that after today, he would not turn his sound notifications back on. He would slowly train himself to live a normal life in his relationship with her. Where had he even gotten these strange tendencies from? It was so unlike him.

He arrived at school and immediately bee lined for his crew's little space in the upper-right corner of the gym. Their clique varied by certain members that moved in and out, but the core of it consisted of Dustin, Steve, Steve's girlfriend, Karissa, Tay, and now Stacy. Stacy was always the first one there due to her being the only walker. Doing a quick inventory, Dustin's heart sank when seeing she was noticeably absent from the group today.

He entered in with them and gave daps to everybody. Steve and Tay were currently in the midst of a debate regarding who was the best boxer of all time: Mike Tyson, or Floyd Mayweather. Steve was arguing for Mayweather due to his lightness and agility. Tay was on the side of Tyson, using his pure aggression and size as his benefits. Dustin stepped in and said the entire argument was null and void because both men were in vastly different weight classes, thus making any hypothetical fight between the two unfair for a multitude of reasons. His friends begrudgingly agreed with him and dropped it, as they usually did when he got involved in such matters.

"Hey, you guys haven't seen Stacy yet, have you?" Dustin was trying to sound as nonchalant as possible.

"Nah, man," Tay said, "unless she's in the morning study hall for some reason. I had to stop in there ten minutes ago to give something to Mr. Parker, and I didn't see her in there."

Dustin nodded.

"All right, Maybe she's sick or something. I'll shoot her a text."

He opened up Messenger. Stacy was still listed as being online. His previous message was still marked as Read.

Hey just checking in Dont see u @ school Msg when you can

He hit send. His message changed to Read immediately. Three periods flashed across the bottom of the thread, then went away. Dustin figured that maybe she'd left her phone open after he texted her earlier. The indicator saying she was typing on and off must have been a glitch. Nothing to worry about.

He decided during morning announcements to leave the sound off but the vibration on. Really, if Stacy was home sick, there wasn't much he could do for her except send her stupid memes or try to make her feel better when he had a minute to do so. The way it looked, she wasn't going to be talking much, anyway.

It was during 3rd period study hall when he felt the vibration in his jean pocket. He looked around for the teacher, but she had apparently stepped out. Feeling safe to do so, Dustin pulled the phone out under the table. He immediately felt better as he saw Stacy's avatar on the screen. Eagerly, he opened the message.

Hey. Sorry, I didn't make it in today. Boss lady seems to have caught a bug. Not much beauty in this rest, but thank you. I was SO nervous calling you handsome. LOL How is your day so far?

He looked around. No sign of Mrs. Phelps yet. Still in the clear.

Aw Im sorry ur not feeling good but I bet you still look gr8! Just in study hall chatting to u U should try 2 get more rest I'm sure you look really beautiful

Ohhhhh, his nerves were running at a thousand miles per second now. Typing, typing. Vibrate. She replied super quickly this time.

With Mrs. Phelps? And you're daring a write-up by having your phone out? You are tempting fate, my cute friend.

She was typing again as soon as that message was sent. The new one:

I'm not beautiful at all. Want me to show you?

Multi-colored sparks flashed behind his eyes. She wanted to send a *picture* of herself? Sure, they saw each other almost every day and had video chatted a few times, but never had they shared anything private for the other one to keep. This really was a big deal. He thought long and hard before he typed out his response.

Haha Ya, risking life and limb just to talk 2 u If I go quiet again its cuz she came back into the room And Im sure you look gr8! Ya, I want 2 see

Looking around, still no teacher. His phone vibrated. He picked it up and almost dropped it from how badly his hands were shaking.

Okay, you asked for it. I warn you, I've definitely seen better days.

Dustin didn't have time to type a response before a thumbnail with a rotating icon came on the screen. A half-portrait of Stacy's tired eyes had just come into view when the classroom door exploded like a gunshot. Dustin snapped his head up. Mrs. Phelps was walking to her desk. Slyly, he put one hand over a book and the other between his legs so he could still hold the phone.

"I hope you're all using this time to study!" Mrs. Phelps called out. "Just a reminder that this is not a time to socialize or do whatever you feel like!"

Idly, Dustin wondered if having her hair tied up in an ultra-tight bun all the time had left Mrs. Phelps with a constant splitting headache. It would at least partially explain her rosy disposition and positive outlook on life. He waited until she pulled out a stack of assignments to grade and looked down at the screen.

Stacy's face stared back at him. Her eyes were red and puffy, and her skin was very pale. She was right in saying she had seen better days, but this did not deter Dustin in the slightest. Rather, it opened up a sympathetic, nurturing side of him that made him wish he were there to help her through the day.

Awwww U still look good Just very sick Is anyone there to help u or are u by urself?

Sent. Read. Mrs. Phelps was still nose-deep in papers. His phone buzzed.

Thank you! I definitely feel like death frozen over. I think I'm going to sleep some more. And no. Mom went to work, and Dad's on a business trip. I'll be okay if I just sleep. Talk to you in a little while. Don't get in trouble with Mrs. Phelps!

Okay.

He hit send. Stacy's active status went away soon after.

Slowly, Dustin wiggled the phone back into his pocket with one hand. He glanced up. No one was looking at him. The room was packed with students, and, for once, they were all utilizing study hall for what it was intended for. Everyone except him. No worries; he probably would be doing the same exact thing even if Stacy were there. This was her swim class period, and she had a lifelong phobia of water. They'd stick people like her in Mr. Parker's classroom to do writing assignments on various topics. She'd usually have hers done before the period was halfway over, sneaking Dustin texts every now and then when Mr. Parker would step out or be distracted. Not that she would get in trouble—Stacy was the intellectual pride and joy of all the teachers at Berthshire High. She could set someone on fire in plain view of everyone and put them out with rock salt. She'd still get cheered and probably be given valedictorian on top of that.

Dustin opened his Geography textbook and set it on the desk. Every minute or so, he'd flip the page, creating the illusion that he was actually reading it. They still had twenty minutes left in the period when he felt his phone buzz against his leg again. Mrs. Phelps was scanning the room now, trying to find the source of the noise. She made a few optical passes and then went back to grading, her eyebrows furrowed in annoyance.

Dustin gave it a little while before slowly sliding the phone out again. He checked the home screen. Stacy. Maybe she wasn't able to sleep. He swiped the message open.

Hey honey. Want to see more pics? I'm feeling a lot better now.

Dustin almost jerked back in his seat. That escalated quickly and unexpectedly. Could she be meaning what he thought she was meaning?

His phone buzzed again.

Please. I really want you to see what I look like right now, followed by a winking face emoji.

He thought, then typed.

Umm…yeah, u can send me more Just remember Im in school haha Don't want both of us 2 get in trouble

Don't worry handsome. You'll really like these.

The first picture loaded. Dustin's arousal turned to confusion. It was Stacy, her head sideways on a stack of pillows.

Her face was still very white, her hair splayed across the top pillow like a fan made of brown silk. Her eyes were closed and her mouth was slightly open, as if she were still asleep. Another message followed the picture.

Like what you see?

Dustin hesitated, then sent a response.

Yeah I guess But how did u take that while u were asleep? Who was holding the phone?

She was immediately typing again. A knot was developing in his stomach. Something about this didn't seem right.

Magic silly. Here's some more to make you feel good. All I want to do is make you feel good.

Another picture loaded. This one was of Stacy's entire body, lying on her bed. She was snuggled underneath a heavy quilt decorated with flowers and foliage. She had switched positions from the first one. Her face was pointed away from the photographer this time. The faintest hint of a shadow loomed over her head and shoulders.

Before he could process what he was seeing, Dustin received yet another photo of her. This time, Stacy's face was back in view. Her eyes were slightly open, as if the picture had been snapped literal seconds after she'd woken up. Another followed after that, and now Dustin actually did jerk back in his chair.

"Mr. Taylor, is there a problem?"

Mrs. Phelps could have been a thousand miles away or shouting directly into his ear with a megaphone; he wouldn't have heard her, either way. He felt himself sliding out of reality. He'd experienced the same sensation in the cornfield after the Trevor-thing had left him there, lying like a baby in the grass, covered in his own urine. He quickly reached up and pinched his own arm to bring himself back. He had to see this, had to accept it. Otherwise, hope for Stacy might be lost. He forced his eyes to look at the image on the screen again.

The settings had changed. It was now what he assumed to

be a dimly lit basement. The walls were made of gray cinder blocks, the floor a bluish gray concrete. In the center of the room was a folding chair, set underneath a bright light. Sitting on the chair was Stacy, still in her white nightgown.

Her limbs were bound with black electrical tape. Her arms were behind her back while her bare feet were on the floor, ankles heavily taped together. Her hair was in her face. Through it, he could see her eyes looking up at the cameraman. They were bloodshot and half-lidded, like a dog that had been heavily tranquilized. Tendrils of dark blood were running from her nose to the silver duct tape that had been wrapped around her mouth to the back of her head. On the right corner of the picture, barely in view, was the end of a large kitchen knife. The three dots appeared at the bottom of the screen. Typing, and then a message.

"Mr. Taylor! I said, is there a problem?"

Dustin stumbled to his feet and walked to the front of the classroom. Twice, he lost all strength in his legs and fell into the desks on his left side. The students sitting at them looked up in surprised irritation and then concern.

"Mr. Taylor! I suggest you take a seat, right this instant!"

He made it to the door and then the hallway. Mrs. Phelps was still yelling at him from behind, demanding he return immediately. Her voice sounded like it was in a faraway echo chamber, bouncing back and forth from his left ear to the right, then back to the left again. A trio of freshmen passed by him. Their faces looked distorted and out of proportion, like monsters trapped in a house of mirrors.

"Heyyyy, broooo. Yooooou okaaaaaaay?"

Dustin shook his head and almost went out of it again. This time, he bit into his tongue until the taste of rusty pennies filled his mouth. He hobbled to the nearest Exit doors and outside, careless of the students and teachers yelling his name from the corridor. He made it to the steps at the front of the building and half sat/half fell onto the top one.

He opened his phone to dial 911. Before he did, the chat thread with Stacy opened one last time. He read the final message again.

You into the rough stuff lil bro?

Stacy's profile was now offline.

CHAPTER 17

Desta was driving around town running errands when she received the call from the police. Dustin had been taken to the station to answer questions regarding a missing person. No, he was not a suspect; no, they could not answer specific questions over the phone; yes, she could come to the Berthshire P.D. ASAP; yes, they would answer what questions they could when she arrived.

She raced there as quickly as she could, which was not long given her speed and how small the town of Berthshire was. Within ten minutes, she was pulling into the municipal parking lot. Two minutes after that, she was in the police station across the street, demanding to see her son.

"He's in the office with the chief, Desta. It would probably be best if you let them finish before goin' in there. This looks pretty serious."

The man she was talking to was the same one she'd spoken with on the phone: Deputy Wayne Tompkins. He was an overweight man in his early forties. They had attended high school together, with him graduating two years ahead of her. His voice still held the stereotypical Appalachian twang that she herself had shed many years ago when she moved up north to Pittsburgh for college. He'd always had a bit of a crush on her, something she'd used to her advantage to get out of parking tickets numerous times. Then, she had flirted with him to get the results she wanted. She was not acting so sweetly right now.

"Damn it, Wayne, what the hell happened?" she demanded. "A missing person's case? What does that have to do with Dustin? He'd never even attempt to hurt anyone."

"It doesn't, at least directly," Deputy Tompkins said in a low voice. "Come with me to the lobby and sit down. I'll fill you in on what I can."

Desta grudgingly followed him into the lobby, taking a seat directly across from him. The police station was located in the basement of the old municipal building, what now served as the town's library. It held a small office, two-single person cells—complete with a pair of plastic bunks, two sinks, and stainless steel toilets with no lids—and a bathroom for employees and visitors. Dustin was currently in the office with the door closed. Desta could see the tops of his and Chief Corna's heads through the caged window ahead of her.

"This morning," Tompkins said, "at around 10:45, a female by the name of Stacy Demeno contacted Dustin through an online messaging app. Are you familiar with that name at all, Desta?"

"Yes," she affirmed. "That's Dustin's girlfriend, although he could probably pass a lie detector test trying to convince you she isn't."

"Okay," Tompkins continued. "As they were talking, her messages became...strange. Not in character with how she was communicating with him before that. Then, a series of increasingly disturbing photos were sent, seemingly taken by an outside party. The final picture was of Stacy, tied to a chair. She appeared to be alive, but badly beaten."

"Oh, my God..." Desta said, her voice wavering. "Did you

find her there, at the house, I mean? Is she…" She stopped before the final word could come out.

"No, she was not at the residence when we arrived. There were small traces of blood on her pillows and blanket. The photo I mentioned was taken from her basement. We found the chair down there, along with the tape used to bind her. Her nightgown had been cut off her body and left at the bottom of the stairs. Apparently, she had stayed home from school today due to some kind of illness. We found some empty DayQuil and Tylenol packs in her bathroom garbage. We don't know where she is or her state at this time."

"And how is Dustin right now? How is he handling all of this?" She unconsciously dug her shaking fingers into her purse and retrieved a Marlboro menthol. She plucked it out and put the filter in her lips.

Though the station had become non-smoking eight years ago, Tompkins reached into his pocket and produced a blue BiC lighter. He flicked the top with his thumb, producing a small orange flame. Desta leaned in as he held it up for her. She took a couple of puffs, sitting back when she was sure the cigarette was properly lit.

"He's distraught," Tompkins said. "He was barely able to talk when we got him in here. I guess he's really sweet on this Demeno girl, ain't he?"

"Yes," Desta said. "He really likes her. You got an ashtray down here so I'm not flickin on the floor?" Tompkins' drawl was bringing out her own dormant accent. She wished she was speaking with Chief Corna right now.

"Sure, just a sec."

Tompkins got up and unlocked the office door. He was back seconds later with a small white ashtray. He passed it to her and sat back down.

"Me and Higgins smoke down here sometimes. We'll let the drunks and tweakers do it, too, if they're far out of their minds enough not to be let outside. The Chief doesn't much like it, but he hasn't raised up too much of a fuss yet."

Darryl Higgins was the town's other full-time deputy. He was younger than Tompkins and *much younger* than the chief, who was flirting with sixty more and more as the days went by. Higgins was in his early to mid-thirties. The flirting Desta had done with him in the past had not come from trying to get out of a parking ticket.

"So," Desta said, "what does Corna think Dustin can tell him that you all don't already know? I feel sorry for Stacy and hope you find her, but it doesn't sound like he has much to do with this at all, beyond being involved with her and receiving the pictures."

"Well…" Tompkins said carefully, choosing his next words with caution. "Based on the messages, we have reason to believe the person who assaulted Stacy may know or know of Dustin. They seemed to be…messing with him, taunting him. Maybe a jealous ex-boyfriend?"

Desta shook her head.

"No. Dustin was her first, just like she was his…first. He talks all the time about how she's never dated before. It's like he's proud of it."

"All right, fair enough. Kids can lie, though, especially girls, if they don't want to come across as too…easy." Tompkins reached under his chair, pulling out a thermos full of coffee. "We just need to talk to him to exhaust every resource, see if there's something we're missin'."

He took a big sip out of the thermos.

"Question for ya, Des."

"Yeah, go ahead." She was finishing up her cigarette.

"You know anyone who calls Dusty any nicknames? Specifically, 'lil bro'?"

"Um, well…" Desta's face had gone printer paper white. "His brother used to call him that a long time ago."

"Trevor. The dead one." Tompkins immediately dropped

his eyes to his shoes. "Too much cop speak. I'm sorry, Des." The deputy had had his fair share of dealings with the elder Taylor boy when he was alive, a fact Desta was well aware of.

"Yes, him. I don't know of anyone else who would call Dustin that."

She stubbed the cigarette and handed the ashtray back to him. As she did, the office door ahead popped open. Chief Corna was standing in the frame.

"Hey, Des. Thanks for letting me have him alone a little longer. Tompkins here fill you in on everything?"

"Yes," she said, collecting her purse off the floor. "Can I go back and see him now? He must be absolutely heartbroken."

Corna nodded. The cords in his neck stood out prominently, and he must have lost fifteen pounds since the last time Desta had seen him. His time of busting wife beaters and chasing down meth heads on the street was clearly running its course.

"Yup, you can go back with him. Keep 'im back there for now, though. There might be a few more things we want to go over before he leaves. Shouldn't keep you more than an hour."

"Thank you, Chief," Desta said, standing up. "I really hope you do find her. She seems like a really sweet girl, and she's so good for Dustin."

"Yes, ma'am," Corna said in his deep drawl. "He's a good boy. We're gonna do everything we can to get her back. Her mother's a nervous wreck, and her daddy's flyin' in all the way from Paris. They're already workin' on posters and talkin' to the news."

"I'm sure they are. I'll...pray for them. Thank you both again." Desta nodded at both of them, then went through the office door.

"Wayne, what did I tell you 'bout smokin' in here? You're going to—"

Desta shut the door behind her, cutting Chief Corna's

voice off. The office was a clutter of papers and folders on three separate desks. One sat up front near the caged-in window, while the other two were further back, set across from one another against the back wall. Dustin was sitting at the far left of these. His skin was pale, and his hair was disheveled. Around his eyes were dark circles. It was clear that he'd been crying.

He looked up as she approached him. For the first time in hours, a semblance of a smile formed on his lips.

"Hi, Mom. Sorry you had to leave work." His voice was hoarse and cracked.

"Hey," she said, grabbing a chair from the other desk and pulling it up beside his. "Hey, no apologizing. It's okay. I was already out early, going around town buying stuff for the house. How are you holding up?"

He choked back a sniffle.

"I don't know, Mom. I really don't know. They tried using the GPS tracker on her phone. They found it on the sidewalk, outside her house. They were hoping her parents had a doorbell cam or something installed to catch what happened, but —he raised both hands in the air, indicating the Demenos had no such system installed—nothing. They called in the FBI to find her. God, this is so, so bad." He began crying.

Wrapping her arm around his shuddering shoulders, Desta leaned in and put her head on the back of his. They sat there like that for a while. Absently, Dustin reached into his pocket to check his phone, only to remember Chief Corna had asked for it so they could examine Dustin and Stacy's conversations for any possible clues. Dustin handed it over, knowing full well they weren't going to find anything. Trevor had been methodical and practical about orchestrating this. He wanted to hit Dustin suddenly and violently, leaving no room for error, and he/it had accomplished exactly that.

"She's going to die, Mom. She's going to die if she isn't dead already, and it's all my fault."

Desta massaged his shoulders gently and kissed the back of his head.

"It's not your fault," she whispered. "How is it your fault? You didn't do anything. Why would you think that?'

He shook his head.

"Just for living. For having a life. Having something."

She was about to inquire further when Chief Corna came back into the room. He had two smartphones in his hand, one in a black case and one in a pink case. He approached them and held the one in the black case out to Dustin.

"Here's your phone, son. You were right, we couldn't find much on it."

Dustin accepted his phone back, staring longingly at the pink one still in Corna's hand.

"What about Stacy's? Nothing on hers?"

"No," the Chief said with a shake of the head. "If we did, I couldn't tell you, of course, but right now, we're lookin' at a whole buncha dead ends. The only lead we have is that he contacted you specifically before he took here. There are no other records showin' anyone else knew about this.

"Son, are you sure you can't think of anyone? A beef at school, one of her pissed off exes that didn't like the idea of you two talkin' so much, something from the past that maybe you forgot and someone else didn't?"

Dustin was shaking his head. Desta examined him closely. His lower lip was clenched firmly in between his teeth.

"No," Dustin said finally. "There's no one. I don't know why anyone would want to hurt her."

"All right," said Corna. "I think that's all I can ask you for right now. We have your number, and I gave you my card. If you think of *anything*, you'll call us?"

Dustin nodded, wiping tears away from his eyes.

"Good. And if we need anything more, we'll call you or give your mom a ring. We're going to find her, son, I promise. We're gonna bring her home."

"Okay," Dustin said, standing up.

"All right. I guess that's all there is for now. Go on home and get yourself some sleep. I need to call Stacy's parents and get them up to date. You know the way out?"

"Yes," Desta said, taking Dustin's hand and guiding him to the door. "Thank you so much, Ed."

Corna shook both of their hands, then made his way to the other desk where the station's lone telephone sat. Desta and Dustin made their way back to the lobby. Deputy Tompkins was in the bathroom, scrubbing out the ashtray he'd given to Desta earlier. The entire room stank of cheap floral air freshener.

"Thanks again, Will," Desta said. "Sorry I got you in trouble."

He looked out at them, offering a small smile.

"Not a problem. He'll get over it. Have a good night, Des. You and your boy will be okay."

"Yes, we will." She gave Dustin's hand a squeeze. "Have a good night."

Tompkins tipped them a slight nod and went back to scrubbing. Desta looked at Dustin. He looked indescribably tired and forlorn, but he was still there mentally. This was good. Him checking out right now would do no good for the situation at all.

They climbed the basement stairs and went outside. It was beginning to get dark. The temperature had dropped thirteen degrees since Dustin was first brought in four hours ago. All he was wearing was a plain red t-shirt and a pair of green sweatpants. He was giving no indication that he was cold at all.

"You have a hoodie in the back of the car," Desta said. "I'm gonna go grab it real quick."

Dustin nodded as they crossed the street and approached the Civic. She went to the back and pulled out his Five Finger Death Punch zip-up. She made her way to the passenger side to hand it to him, only to discover Dustin wasn't there.

"Over here," he called from across the car. She looked over, confused.

"What are you doing, sweetheart? I don't think it's a good idea for you to drive right now, baby."

"I can drive," he said, an eerily calm cadence to his voice, considering the circumstances. "I have something I need to tell you, but I can't until you see first."

"See what?" Desta said. Despite having a bad feeling about what this might entail, she pulled her keys from her purse and tossed them to him.

"Thank you. You'll see what I mean when I show you."

They got in and pulled out. Dustin made a left out of the parking lot and headed down First Street for one mile, then hung a right at Yorkshire Road. They passed by the old elementary school he used to attend, now condemned, with boarded-up windows and graffiti all along the exterior. It was desolate out here, with mostly open farmland and the occasional house off in the distance.

Dustin looked away as they passed by the liquor store that had been built out here four years ago. It had just reopened one week ago after the robbery last month. (Chief Corna had also investigated that case. No one had been questioned about it, and no suspects had been found).

Up ahead was a tall metal archway, decorated with child-like cherubs all along the sides. Below that was a paved road, surrounded by gravestones. Desta suddenly felt very sick.

"Sweetie, what are we doing out here?"

A clicking noise was heard as Dustin flicked the blinker to go to the right.

"We're going to visit Trevor's grave. Please don't fight me about this. I really need you to see. For us *both* to see."

He braced himself, ready for screaming protests and an emotional tirade. Anything regarding Trevor set Desta off, especially if it involved discussing or even acknowledging his death or the circumstances surrounding it. So, then, Dustin was surprised when Desta responded with a simple and unemotional "Okay," saying nothing else after that.

Continuing on, he drove until the big flag pole marking the World War 2 section came into view. Someone had already taken the flag down for the evening. Even after all the years of being away, it still seemed odd to Dustin to see naked blue sky at the top.

He pulled into the grass on the left-hand side and cut the engine. He took in a big breath, then turned to Desta.

"Mom," Dustin said, "whatever we're about to see, I need you to stay calm, okay? If Stacy's still alive, I may need your help, so please, try to keep it together."

Desta kept her eyes on his as he spoke, nodding along. She fingered a cigarette out of her purse and opened the door.

"I don't know why we're out here, or what you're trying to prove," she said, "but I trust you. You're all I have left in this world, and I'll follow you anywhere you need me to go. So, let's go."

She stepped out of the car and slammed the door before he had a chance to respond. He slid the hoodie over his head and arms, zipping it up. Then, he followed her into the sea of granite headstones.

They walked for a few minutes until they came to the final row. On the far end to their left was a tiny headstone, barely visible among the much larger ones surrounding it. This is where they were headed now.

A cold breeze hit them from the west as they approached the grave. Etched onto the front, the stone read:

Trevor Taylor
  Beloved son and brother
  February 21st, 1992-August 17th, 2009

. . .

As they got closer to the marker, both Dustin's and Desta's breathing grew heavier and heavier. When they finally arrived, Dustin stopped breathing altogether for a moment. When it resumed, it was accompanied by heavy, hitching sobs.

The ground before them lay undisturbed. Slightly discolored grass lined the area where Trevor was buried in a faint rectangle, three feet wide at the top and bottom, and six feet long on the sides. A passerby wouldn't even notice the discrepancy if it were in a different location. If anything had dug its way up from underneath the soil, it hadn't done so in a very long time.

"No," Dustin said in a near-whisper. "He was there with me the night I took the car. In the cornfield. At Stacy's He was there. He...was fucking...*THERE!*"

He stomped over to the headstone and kicked the area that had Trevor's first name embedded into it as hard as he could. A swirl of dust wafted into the wind as he screamed incoherently over and over again until his vocal cords felt like they'd be doused in gasoline and set on fire.

Desta ran to his side and grabbed his arm, ardently trying to pull him away. This time, her strength wasn't enough, and she toppled backwards, falling directly into the middle of the rectangle.

"*Dustin!*" she shouted. "*Dustin, goddamn it, STOP!*"

But he wouldn't stop. He stood there for a good ten minutes, screeching obscenities at God, at Trevor, at himself. Ghostly plumes of his breath snaked into the air as he finally had no more words to say. He kneeled at Trevor's grave, sobbing and hugging the headstone. Desta approached him and placed a timid hand on his shoulder—the same one Trevor had grabbed hard enough to leave finger marks in the month before.

"Enough," she said, calmly now. "Trevor's dead, and he's never coming back. Let's go to the car and go home. Maybe one of us has some news about Stacy."

There was no reaction from him until the mention of Stacy's name. At that, Dustin pulled himself up and walked with Desta through the graveyard. It was nighttime now. He felt no sense of fear waltzing amongst the dead. He'd already done that, and so much more, and he would again very soon. With the father he'd never met. With Stacy. With the crickets. It didn't matter. It would all be over soon.

Just then, Dustin said a prayer, begging whatever was in control over the universe to let him stay dead, to never allow him to inflict the kind of terror and pain he had experienced on anyone, in this life or the next. He looked up to the sky, asking for these things in the same way he had asked for Trevor to come back to life six years ago. This time, the Void turned its ear to his pleas, remaining indifferent.

"I love you, Dustin," his mother said as they floated through the darkness together.

"I love you, too," Dustin said, meaning it more than he ever had in his entire life, knowing this might be the final time they would be able to say it to each other.

CHAPTER 18

They arrived at the house and immediately went their separate ways. Dustin headed straight to his room and called his work, notifying them he couldn't make any of his shifts for the rest of the week, also adding that he could not cover for anyone. The evening shift manager responded curtly, thanking Dustin for letting them know, then hung up on him before he could say anything else. He didn't care. He had nothing else he wanted to say, and he didn't have that much concern over what they thought. He was mentally, spiritually, and emotionally exhausted.

He lay in bed for a long time, staring at the home screen on his phone, pretending that it was twenty-four hours ago, visualizing that he and Stacy were in the midst of some silly conversation, and that she'd message him any second with one of her witty replies. He tried to think that she was about to randomly call him, as she did sometimes, to tell him about her day, or something she was thinking about. Ten minutes, twenty minutes, forty minutes, two hours. Nothing but deafening silence.

He was still lying there when Desta knocked on his door.

Iron Fist was not present tonight; she knocked gently and slowly, not wanting to startle him if he was sleeping. Nor did she yell out his name as she usually did, instead standing patiently at the door until he gave his permission to enter.

"Come in, Mom," he said quietly.

The door opened. In Desta's hand was a steaming mug of cocoa and a packet of Tylenol. She sat down at the foot of his bed and held the two items out to him. He accepted both, taking them from her and placing them on his nightstand.

"Thanks, Mom. I'll let it cool down for a couple of minutes. The Tylenol will help, too."

"I put marshmallows in it," Desta said shyly. "I know you're almost an adult now, but you used to really like for me to do that when you were little. You'd use a spoon and make them into a little smiley face or a heart. It was sweet."

Dustin nodded and picked up the cup, sipping on it gently so it didn't burn his tongue. A lone marshmallow made it through his lips. He caught it with his back teeth and bit down, savoring the sweet flavor. Some deep part of his subconscious remembered the times Desta was speaking of, sitting in the house when school was out for a snow day, drinking hot cocoa and playing board games with her and Trevor. Before the drugs, before the death, before the Bad Thing, whatever that was. But things had gotten better since all of that happened, so why this? Why now?

"Dustin," Desta said while he drank. "I don't know what Trevor did to you when you were younger. I know some of it, but not all, and probably not even the worst of it. And that's okay, I don't need to know. What's done is done, and can't be changed. Are you understanding me so far?"

He nodded. His eyes looked dead and soulless. Absently, he moved the spoon around the cup to form a face with the marshmallows, just like he used to do as a kid. The only difference was, this face had furrowed eyebrows and a scowl at the mouth rather than a smile. Half a mouth—the other half had been blown off in a meth lab explosion.

"Okay. Honey, Trevor is gone. And when he left us, we had each other. I don't want to say it, but Stacy might be gone now, too. I pray to Jesus she isn't, but if she is, we'll still have each other. We always will. You understand that, too, right?"

"Yeah," he said. "Thanks, Mom. I know I'll always have you."

"And you know that I'd never turn you away or leave you alone," she continued. "You or Trevor. He may have had many problems, but he was still my son, just like you are. If I could have stopped what happened..." Desta choked back a sob. "If I could have done something to save him, I would have. I kept him here, tried to reason with him, forgave him over and over again when a lot of parents wouldn't have. He needed me, just like you need me. Just always know I love you as much as I do him, okay?"

"Okay, Mom." He was finishing up the cocoa now. "Where's yours at?"

"Where's my what, my love?"

"Your cocoa," he said. "I walked past the kitchen a little while ago to get my charger, and you had two mugs out on the counter."

"Oh," she said, "I drank mine while I was waiting for yours to brew."

"I hope you didn't burn your mouth." Dustin's eyes were slitted. He was barely able to keep them open.

She flashed him a small smile.

"No, sweetie, I didn't. I'm going to let you go to bed now, okay?" Desta stood up. She was already in her nightgown for the evening. "Come to me if you need me for anything, okay?"

"Okay, Mom."

Desta left him and went to her room. She pulled her comforter down and crawled underneath it. Five minutes later, there was a soft tapping at her door. It did not rouse her; she'd been lying there, wide awake, anticipating this. She closed her eyes a little as the door creaked open.

"Yeah, sweetie?" she said sleepily.

"Mom?" Dustin asked in a child-like voice. "Is it okay if, um…I mean, would it be all right if…"

"Of course, baby," she said, pulling the comforter down and scooching over to make space on the bed. "Come on, it's okay."

Dustin crawled beside her. Moments later, he was lightly snoring. Sometime during the night, he rolled over and draped his arm across her shoulders. Desta lay there in the dark, her lips curled into a contented smile.

CHAPTER 19

Dustin did not go to school the next morning. Desta called in herself, telling them he'd come down with a winter bug and may need to be out for the rest of the week. He slept in her bed till well past noon. She did not attempt to wake him before she left for work in the morning.

When Dustin did wake up, he was greeted with an orange Post-It note pasted to her vanity mirror, telling him there were eggs and sausage in the refrigerator, and that she had fresh clothes and a towel out for him in the bathroom. He went to his room to check his phone. No new messages, no missed calls. He felt the pain cutting through him again as he forced himself to take a shower and then eat. He glanced at the X-Box when he entered the living room, not giving it a second thought.

The familiar place he'd lived in all his life felt like a faraway continent now. The sun beaming in through the windows—normally a comforting and delightful sight—felt overwhelming, creating a form of sensory overload that made him sick to look at. The light was an illusion, everything it shone upon some decaying, dying thing that hadn't reached its full potential yet and never would, rotting just like the tractor at Aunt Cindy's farm—forgotten, disused, valueless. That's what the world was, what *he* was. After all, he'd been bred to be that way.

He forced himself to call the police station. It was Higgins who answered. No, they hadn't had any updates on Stacy's whereabouts; no, they didn't have any leads; yes, they would call him immediately if they had any updates. After he hung up, Dustin texted his mom, thanking her for the breakfast. That old surge of endorphins pulsed through him a minute later when his phone *Dinged!* with her response.

Of course baby. Anything you need. You want me to come home? I can leave Sheila and Mary here. It's slow today.

Dustin told her she didn't need to do that and that he'd be okay. Desta replied, telling him to call her if he needed her, followed by a line of emojis with hearts on the faces. This brought Dustin a great sense of comfort, and he hated himself for it. It was like simulating a conversation with Stacy and replacing her with his own mother. The very thought of it made him sick to his stomach.

It would be hours until Mom would be home. He absolutely dreaded the prospect of sitting around, doing nothing until then, especially with Stacy still out there. He'd decided after waking up that Trevor had not killed her; it wasn't even a possibility; it couldn't even be entertained as a hypothetical. Dustin was the only person in the world who knew who had taken her, and he was the only one who could save her. And he would, come Hell or high water. He was done being afraid of Trevor. He just needed to think of what he could do about it.

He was outside the storage room door now, hyping himself up. If there was any chance of finding an answer to anything, it would be in there. To his knowledge, Trevor had only been in the house for two nights. There might not be anything in there at all, but it was the only place he could think of looking after checking the grave the day before. He looked at the door one last time, mentally prepping for what he might find on the other side. He took a deep breath, said a brief prayer, and then went in.

Some of the totes had been moved since the last time he'd entered the room. This did not surprise nor alarm him. As if fulfilling a prophecy, Mom had been in here a few days after he put everything back from the Thanksgiving incident, restoring it to whatever insane mental organization that made sense to her and her alone. Starting off with it exactly as it should be this time afforded him the ability to take internal note of where everything was supposed to go after he was done—not that such a trivial thing mattered, but at least it gave his brain something to focus on rather than constantly worrying.

Immediately, he headed over to the totes near the far back window—the one Trevor had used to enter and exit the house. He sucked his gut in and scooted between the wall and the clutter until he reached the ones that had Trevor's name written on them in black marker. He pulled a couple of totes off, picking up the one from the very bottom, marked *Trevor, 13-17, misc.* Dustin himself had three totes dedicated to his belongings in this age range. Once the drugs had started, Trevor required less and less in regards to material possessions, pawning or straight up selling the most expensive items he owned in order to support his ever-increasing habits.

Dustin put the tote on an old wooden end table next to him and started rummaging inside. In it, he found old posters of various hip-hop artists from the time period, CDs in slip cases, a few books that looked like they'd never been opened, and a couple of boxes of Choreboy cleaners. Beyond that, nothing.

He put everything back in and set it aside, grabbing the

tote that was on top of that one and setting it on the table. This one was marked *Trevor, 13-17, clothes*. It was much heavier than the previous one. He almost needed to toss it onto the table just to get it up. He opened the lid.

An odor of stale fabric softener and moth balls wafted towards his nose as he leaned down. Trevor's clothes were folded neatly, pants and underwear on the left, shirts and socks on the right. Immediately, Dustin noticed how the socks and underwear on top were in slight disarray—from when Trevor had dug in there to get his Tupac shirt and cargo shorts.

Piece by piece, Dustin took the articles out and stacked them on top of one another, being careful not to sully Desta's department store-level folding job. Small clods of dirt fell to the floor as he searched, reminding him of Trevor's initial state when he first arrived. Halfway through, he found a liquor bottle cap, still wet with residue on the inside. Beyond these small indicators of Trevor's recent presence, another dead end. He carefully placed the clothes back as they were, then returned the totes to the same arrangement he had found them in.

Feeling dejected and hopeless, Dustin looked around the room, trying to think if there was anything else he could check. Trevor had gotten into the decoration bins, but was there anything else he might have looked through? The entire room had been rearranged that night. It could have literally gotten into *anything* without it being detected. Dustin originally possessed a hope that being shown Stacy's state had been more than just an attempt to psychologically toy with him, that maybe Trevor was using her as bait to lure him in for some kind of final confrontation. The last photo had shown her in a dismal state—beaten, bound, terrified, but still very much alive. The police had her phone; Trevor had no way to contact him anymore. So, why had it sent a picture of her alive just to kill her and have Dustin never know? There had to be a clue somewhere. Why wouldn't there be?

Because he—it—is insane, that calm internal voice reminded him. Remember what you told yourself the last time you were in here, how the sane way to see a junkie's perspective is to toss sanity out the window? You saw those eyes. This is that insanity taken to an extreme you can't comprehend. She's dead, and he's coming for you next. There's nothing you can do about it, so just accept it.

"Fuck that," he told himself. "No, I'm done with his shit. I was done with it when I was a kid, and I'm not doing it again now. Just *think*, Dustin, fucking *think*."

Trevor had talked to him at the ranch and on the night of the Hell ride. Dustin played through what he could remember of the conversations, seeing if he could recall anything that might indicate where the living corpse was hiding now.

Disparaging comments regarding Dustin and Desta…the "joy rides" they used to take…Mark and John…Was there *anything* else?

Mom used to take me horse riding back when I was a kid.

Dustin remembered a conversation Mom and Aunt Cindy had had as he was getting ready to mount Black Velvet. Mom had told him about the last time the family was there, and how Trevor had his own riding boots at the time. Aunt Cindy's face seemed to have changed for a moment at the mention of his name, her otherwise youthful features sagging down into a scowl, making her look much older than she actually was. Cindy had changed the subject abruptly, seemingly not wanting to discuss Desta's other son in the slightest. Could that be a possible clue?

Going off of instinct more than anything else, Dustin slid himself out to the front of the room and made his way over to the other side, where the photos were. He looked through the boxes on top. It didn't take him long to find the one marked *Trevor*. While the other boxes were mid-sized and in fairly good condition, this one was small and puffed out on the sides, the edges looking like they were going to break at even the slightest mishandling. He carefully picked it up by the sides and carried it over to another discarded end table. Immediately, he saw the remnants of fingerprints on the top folds. Dirt. Trevor had looked through it.

He opened it. A pile of glossy photographs stared back at him. Mom had clearly put the box back without looking through it first. A combination of Polaroids with yelling edges and newer photos developed at a photo center were mixed together in a chaotic jumble.

In one picture, there was Trevor on a wooden riding horse. He was shirtless and couldn't have been more than four years old. He was wearing a brown plastic cowboy hat with a painted-on buckle in the center. In the background, sitting on a couch Dustin had never seen before, was their father. He was dressed in a pair of faded blue jeans with a rip in one knee and an olive green t-shirt that had Marines stenciled across the left breast pocket in bold black lettering. Both he and Trevor were sporting wide, cheesy grins. Trevor's hair was still a thick dark brown, not yet lightening to the wispy dishwater blond Dustin had known him to have years later. His older brother's eyes were wide and sparkling, as if they had an eternity of life behind them.

The one underneath that was of Trevor when he was much older, maybe thirteen or fourteen. In this instance, his eyes were squinted and puffy, his cheeks a deep crimson. He was standing outside a McDonald's drive-thru sometime at night. He was adorned in a heavy black hoodie and bright orange Nike shorts. Leaning back against someone's car, he had both hands up near his chest with his fingers splayed, his upper lip in a pucker. It almost looked like a pose from one of the rappers on his hip-hop posters.

Dustin sifted through more of the photos. He found some of him and Trevor, mostly before Trevor was a teenager. The earlier ones were innocent enough. While the seedlings of his older brother's downward spiral were evident as his expression progressed to more and more dour and withdrawn, the brothers looked genuinely happy to be in each other's company. Whether it was Trevor pushing toddler Dustin down a small plastic slide or the two of them spraying each other with hoses in Grandma and Grandad's old backyard in Wheeling, the two boys always seemed to be laughing and joyful together.

The later pictures, though…the faces in those told a much different story. While Trevor would still be smiling and jovial, Dustin would be expressionless and looking downward, clearly uncomfortable with the lack of physical space between them. While Trevor looked in good spirits on the surface level, there was an underlying aura of malicious menace in his face. His hair was becoming thinner and more manic, his teeth more flaxen and spaced apart as the years went by. By the end, he looked like a mad scientist, aged well beyond his years. Dustin was not present in these photos. Desta was actively trying to keep them apart at this point. Trevor had already received an underage DUI charge and had run away from one juvenile detention facility, along with being kicked out of two others.

Dustin fought against his conflicting emotions and searched further until he finally found what he was looking for. He pulled out a stack of Polaroids in a rubber band and walked them over to where the light was spilling in through the window to get a better look.

Aunt Cindy's house was recognizable right away. There was a green porch swing that wasn't there anymore, and the white paint looked brighter and a little cleaner, but Dustin was certain this was the same place he had visited with Mom less than a month before.

Trevor stood front and center under the bright sunlight. In this one, he was probably between the ages of ten and eleven. He was on the sidewalk leading up to the house, wearing a pair of denim overalls with a long-sleeved white and red plaid shirt underneath. This brought forth memories of Dustin's nightmares of the same being riding the John Deere tractor, chasing him down in the cornfield. He shivered.

Trevor's small thumbs were poking out from his clenched fists. His smile in this one was broken by a missing left tooth that would grow back in sideways, requiring braces for the following year and a half. Behind him was a tall black horse—not Black Velvet, the one Dustin had ridden, but one that looked very similar.

Dustin pulled this picture out and put it at the bottom of the pile. The next one was of Trevor and Aunt Cindy. It looked like it was from the same day based on what Trevor was wearing. They were standing in front of a building Dustin didn't recognize—probably the old barn that had burnt down. Mom told him about it on their way up to Somerset.

Trevor was sitting on top of the horse from the previous picture. Aunt Cindy was on the left side of him, looking up and laughing at something he was saying. Desta must have been the one behind the camera.

The picture underneath that caused him to give pause. Same day. Trevor was still in suspenders and the plaid shirt. This one was taken near sundown. The background was a warm orange, similar to the day Dustin had been there. Off in the distance, he could see the cornfield. Yellow coronas of sunflowers lined the entire front, many more than had been there when he visited.

Trevor wasn't smiling in this one. The best way to describe his demeanor was blank. He looked more like the Trevor in his teenage years than the laughing, happy little boy in the older photos from the same time period. There was no one else in the frame.

Dustin moved to the next picture. He felt his pulse begin to thump in his ear. His skin was suddenly cold and clammy.

Trevor was in his underwear. The suspenders and shirt lay on the ground a few feet away from him. His mouth was open, as if he were in the middle of saying something right when the snapshot had been taken. His face was burning red, covered in big oily teardrops. To the right, barely in the periphery of the frame, was the black nose of the horse from the earlier pictures.

Dustin let out a gasp when he switched to the next-to-last picture. Now his pulse was *drumming* throughout his neck and temples. He tasted a cocktail of sewage and stomach acid in his mouth as raw bile rose to the back of his throat.

The horse lay on its side. The soil beside it was covered in a pool of blood. Small bubbles were visible in the middle of the puddle. A wide trail of darker dirt snaked up to the horse's neck, which had been slit from ear to ear. Beside the head lay a rusty machete, the blade and side sheening with the same liquid.

Sitting behind the horse's body was Trevor. His white briefs were now stained with deep red hand prints. His legs, arms, chest, neck, and face were also smeared with it, as if he had gotten it on his hands and tried to use his own skin to clean it off. Even without the benefit of sound, Dustin could hear him wailing in the photograph, the look of horrified hysterics on the small child's face enough to create a shrieking loop of audio that made his ears feel as if they were going to blow out from the side of his head.

Shuddering and trying not to retch, Dustin switched to the final photograph. It was back in front of Cindy's house. This was the only picture that had Desta in it. She was kneeling on the front deck, holding a crying Trevor as Cindy watched on from the side, a look of mortified concern on her face.

Desta was wearing a white and orange sundress. It was streaked all over with patches of light red from Trevor's body.

She had her arms wrapped around him as he had his head buried into her shoulder, much in the same way Dustin had done with her multiple times in the past month. Her eyes were closed and her lips were pressed together in a thin line. Dustin could almost hear the words she was whispering right at that moment.

"Shh, shh. Calm down, baby, it's all right. Mommy's here for you, and I won't ever leave you. Anything you need, honey, I'm here."

It was only now that Dustin noticed the vantage point in the pictures. While the first two were taken from the height of a short adult—probably Desta—the final three were closer to ground level and pointed upward, as if the photographer had to tilt the camera in order to get everything in frame—even Trevor, who couldn't have been more than eleven years old, stood taller, though not by much. He'd always been on the shorter side, even then.

Dustin was preparing to move the final picture to the bottom of the pile when he saw something odd. At the very bottom of the Polaroid was a smudge of blue ink on the white flap. He flipped the photo over, but found nothing on the opposite side. He pulled out the previous one with the dead horse on it and checked the back. This one had a note written on it in jittery handwriting.

Family Time, 2004

DING!

Dustin screamed and jumped backwards, knocking over the box.

On my way home sweetie. I'm bringing McDonald's and some ice cream. I hope you're feeling better. Maybe we can put up some posters for Stacy's parents later tonight?

He stuffed the phone back into his pocket and quickly picked up the pictures on the floor, stuffing them into the box. He put it back as he had found it and left the room, slamming the door shut behind him. Then, he sprinted to the bathroom, throwing the toilet seat up and dropping to his knees. Instantly, a stream of hot, burning vomit shot out through his esophagus, splattering against the lid of the seat and the floor ahead of him. Guttural screaming emerged in between each regurgitation, causing the quiet house to come alive in a cacophony of pain and sickness.

He hung over the commode on his elbows, weak and unable to move. There was a slamming noise on the other end of the house, followed by the muffled jingling of keys.

"Dustin! I'm home, sweetie! I brought Big Macs from McDonald's!"

Dustin gagged again and lay his head on the seat.

CHAPTER 20

They sat in the living room, eating a pair of Dairy Queen hot fudge sundaes, watching *America Says*. Desta was sitting beside Dustin on the couch. This had become the norm since the failed coffee date with Cindy's friend. The recliner had been vacant for days.

Every spoonful of ice cream slid down Dustin's throat like artificially sweetened snot. He'd managed to scarf down the sandwiches from McDonald's, but just barely, quietly dry heaving the bites down when Desta would look away for a moment. All he could think of when chewing the patties was that he was being fed horse meat. The strings of shredded lettuce would get stuck between his teeth, eliciting imagery of course, black hair wrapped all along his gums. It had taken everything within him to hold it down so he didn't upset or offend his mother. She was looking out for him, after all.

When Dustin was finished eating, Desta packed all of his trash in the McDonald's bag and took it to the trash for him. When she came back, he was sitting upright with his hands at his sides. The TV had been turned off.

"What's the matter, sweetie?" she asked. "Did the food upset your stomach?"

Dustin met her eyes and did not look away. This made Desta very nervous.

"What happened in 2004, at Cindy's ranch?"

"Baby, what are you talking about?" Her initial apprehension was developing into something much more severe.

"With Trevor. A horse died, the one he was riding that day. Someone killed it. I saw the pictures."

Desta bit down on her lower lip and took her eyes away from his piercing gaze. She tried to reach for the cigarettes in her pocket, but met nothing but fabric and lint balls. She'd left them in the car.

"I saw pictures," Dustin said. "What happened there? Who did it? Was it Trevor? He would have been too short to reach it. It looked like someone was punishing him for something."

"I'm starting to feel sick," Desta said. "Can I sit down?" All hints of cheery motherly warmth and goodwill were gone from her voice now, replaced by an emotionless monotone.

Dustin nodded to the recliner. Something flashed through her face when he did this—maybe hurt, even a small bit of indignation? Still, she did as he requested, walking over and taking a seat on the recliner.

"You don't remember anything from that year?" she said in that same drone-ish intonation.

"No. I remember going to Dad's funeral, the trip we took to Disneyland in the summer, starting elementary school. But nothing like that. It made me want to puke."

"Where did you find the pictures?"

"In the storage room. Trevor's room. It never stopped being that, did it? Not really."

"I can't believe he kept those," she said more to herself than to Dustin. "That sick son of a bitch bastard. Even from beyond the grave, he's still tormenting me."

"Trevor?" Dustin asked."

"No. *Him*. Craig. You really don't remember, do you?"

Dustin shook his head. "No, I don't. Who's Craig?"

The name sounded vaguely familiar, like how someone sees something and swears it evokes a memory from a past life. A blurry image was there, but not enough to form a clear image.

"Craig Jefferson," Desta said, "was the man I was with after your father. They were good friends from the service, and Norm—your dad—got him a job at the insurance company he worked for. He came out with us to the farm that day. Your father had been gone for five months."

"Was he the one who killed the horse? Why? If a horse gets hurt or gets rabies or something, aren't you, you know, supposed to shoot it in the head, something humane?" He remembered the other part of the photograph just now, with Trevor in his underwear, covered in blood.

"The horse wasn't hurt," Desta said. "We were having a cookout. Uncle Jeff was in the backyard. Me and Cindy were out in the old barn. We left you both with Craig. You were just wrestling around with your brother, and Craig had watched you guys a thousand times before. We didn't think there was anything to worry about."

"Did he kill the horse?" Dustin said bluntly.

"We didn't know it at the time, but yes. He took you and Trevor out near the cornfield while everyone wasn't paying attention. We noticed you both were gone after a little while. He—Desta choked back a sob—said he took you to see the corn. Then, he said you—she pointed at Dustin—ran off, and he had to go chasing after you. He caught you and came back. Then he found Trevor covered in blood and the horse dying. He said he grabbed you both and ran back to the house. You had your little camera with you. That was where the pictures came from. I never went through the whole stack to see them all." She inhaled deeply, taking a long breath.

"And you dated this creep, let him around us after that? Was Dad even buried yet?" Deep down, Dustin felt an ember of anger inside of him that was quickly growing by the second.

"Yes," Desta said with her eyes on her feet. "I didn't start seeing Craig until two months after your father passed. He was so good with you, and with Trevor…" She hesitated. "With Trevor…he was fair, or at least did a good job of making it look that way. What he did, though…"

Dustin's gaze was still locked firmly on her.

"What did he do?"

"He…Did a bad thing. A very Bad Thing." Now she was crying.

"Trevor was in his underwear in these pictures, before the horse was cut. I was there with them, I didn't run away. Did this guy…*do* things to Trevor?"

Sniffling and wiping her eyes, Desta tried to speak, but could only manage to get out a stifled "mmm-hmm" before she completely broke down.

The fire inside of Dustin instantly died. He quickly got up and went to her. Gently, he guided her off the recliner and walked her to the couch, where he sat down with her and hugged her. He himself began crying.

"I just want to find her, Mom. That's all I want. That's how I found those pictures. I was trying to find something. A clue. I just want this whole fucked up thing to stop, for Trevor to stop. But I can't figure out how."

She pulled her face away from his shoulder.

"What do you mean, 'for Trevor to stop'? Is this about what happened yesterday at the graveyard?"

"Yes," he said. "The person who made me take the car last month wasn't some random homeless guy who broke in. I don't know how or why, but Trevor is back. I saw him at Aunt Cindy's. That's what really happened that day. He told me we were gonna go on a joy ride that night, then he woke me and made me go. I fought him and got away. I don't know where he is now."

Desta measured him carefully. He was still looking directly at her. No lip biting. He was telling her the 100% truth on what he perceived to have happened.

"Baby…" she said. "I thought maybe yesterday you had a breakdown because of everything happening. That's why I didn't say much about it. But you really believe this, don't you?"

"Yeah," he said. "That's what happened. He's pissed I lived, and he didn't. He hates that I have you, and he doesn't. He has Stacy, and he is probably going to kill her. Then, he's going to kill me and you. I have to do something."

"Dustin, what you're saying…it's literally impossible." She slowly let go of him. Somehow, her face didn't match the words she was saying. She *sounded* scared, but she looked threatened in a way, bordering on angry.

"I know," he said, speaking quickly now. "There was nothing at the grave. But maybe…I don't know, he crawled out before they buried the casket? Like, living outside this whole time, plotting his revenge."

"Dustin."

"He's dead. Dead people don't need to eat. I know he *can* eat. I found a turkey leg he stole from Thanksgiving. If Stacy is alive, they have to be somewhere outdoors."

"*Dustin.*"

"He's had a lot of time to plan. Maybe he found some-where—an abandoned house, one of the old gas stations on Yorkshire. Actually…holy shit, Mom! The old school! That would be the *perfect* place for him to—"

"*DUSTIN!*"

The force behind her scream shocked him into silence.

"If what you are saying could happen," Desta said, "some-how, someway—if there was some voodoo that could make such a thing possible—no, you know what, I can't even enter-tain this. You need help. You're sick." She pulled out her phone.

"No, no, no, no," he said, reaching out. "Mom, what are you doing?"

She pulled the phone away and stood up, speed walking across the room to the hallway. Dustin followed her. Her pattering footsteps turned into forceful stomps as she sprinted to her bedroom and slammed the door. Dustin arrived just as she engaged the lock on the other side.

"Mom!" He pounded on the door. "Mom, please don't! Listen to me, *please*!"

He pressed his ear against the wood.

"Yes, my name is Desta Taylor. I live at 3122, Center Street. Berthshire. Yes."

"Mom, stop!"

"I have a seventeen-year-old son who is experiencing a psychotic break, possibly due to drugs. I'm locked in my bedroom right now."

"Let me in! Mom, please, don't do this!" He pounded on the door some more. A light brown lightning bolt appeared down the center as the wood began to crack.

"Yes, that's him. No, I'm not in any danger right now, at least, I don't think so, but I've never seen him like this. No, I don't know what he might be on. My other son who passed away had an addiction problem, and he would act in a similar way. Crystal meth. Uh-huh, okay. Just tell them not to hurt him when they get here. He really is a sweet kid."

"Mooo-ooo-ooooom! No! Don't let them take me away! God, please!"

She'd just been crying on his shoulder a minute ago. She knew he would never hurt her. Why was she doing this?

"Paranoid, hallucinating. I'll wait, yes."

Dustin knocked on the door some more, but got no response. Panicking, he looked around in all directions, trying to think of what to do. The back door led to a patch of woods that spanned a mile or so. If he was going to get away, that would be his best choice. He ran to the foyer and slipped his shoes on, then made his way to the kitchen and out the back.

He went around the house through the backyard to the tree line. The frosted grass crunched under his shoes as he entered the woods. He ran blindly for a few minutes until he was deep enough in that he was sure no one would see him. There was a moment where he considered pulling out his phone and using the flashlight, but now there was the squalling of sirens not too far off in the distance. He couldn't risk bringing attention to himself.

Not knowing what direction he was headed in, Dustin continued straight ahead. It was well below freezing now, and all he had on was a thin long-sleeved shirt and basketball shorts. He'd run through a thicket of pricker bushes sometime during the mad dash from the house. His bare legs were stinging from a mixture of the air and the cuts.

As he walked, he thought. Desta had seen him in the graveyard the night before. She'd seen how he reacted whenever he saw Trevor's resting place undisturbed. She never questioned why they were there, or why he had said the things he had about Trevor being with him the month before. He'd been acting much more erratically during that outburst, and her response had been to take him home and make cocoa. She'd even let him sleep with her, which greatly unnerved him now that he was thinking about it clearly.

Tonight, he had calmly said the same things, and it was like a switch was flicked within her. It was as if when he needed her, she was soothing and nurturing, willing to give him a shoulder to cry on—in fact, sometimes *over* willingly. He could say any crazy sounding thing in the world, and it was okay, as long as he needed her. But the second he focused on things outside the two of them, all of his problems were suddenly a threat, and she had to regain control over him by any means necessary.

Nearing the end of the woods, Dustin stopped in a

clearing to catch his breath and evaluate his options. One was to go back to the house and get taken to the hospital. Not gonna happen; he wasn't crazy, even if recent events had made him both feel and look that way at times.

The next thing he could do was move on, investigate some of the things he'd mentioned earlier, like the old gas stations and abandoned school. The problem with this course of action was that Yorkshire Road was six miles away from where he was. He had no coat, no long pants, no vehicle, and it was probably nearing ten degrees now. He'd have hypothermia before morning came.

The third option? Do absolutely nothing. Just sit out here, accept fate, and freeze to death. Stacy dies, Trevor wins, nobody ever knows what happened. As simple as moving forward with this plan sounded, he couldn't fail Stacy—if she was even still out there, which he believed she was.

He was mulling over these options when Hulk Hogan's *Real_American* theme song blasted out from his pocket. He pulled the phone out and held it up to his eyes. He had to squint to read the screen due to light deprivation.

Mom

Doing something he never normally did, Dustin placed his finger on the red circle beneath her name, swiping left to silence the call. His phone started blaring again a few seconds later. Denied. This time, he held the volume button on the side so it stopped making noise and possibly giving away his location.

He was putting the phone back in his pocket when it buzzed just once in his palm. Not another call—a text or voice message. He opened the home screen, seeing it was the former. Not wanting to, he raised his frozen finger and opened it. Of course, it was from Mom. Who else would be trying to talk to him? She was all he had.

Please call me. EMTs are gone. I need to talk. Come home. PLEASE!

Dustin didn't know what to do. As he was thinking, another text came through.

Honey I believe you. I found something here. Please, call me.

Could he be tracked for a call from one cell phone to another? If he were a missing person or a suspect of a major crime, definitely. But in small town Berthshire, at this time of night, for a mental health check? He highly doubted it. Taking his chances, Dustin pushed the call icon next to Desta's name and placed the phone to his ear. It rang twice before she answered.

"Baby? *BABY*! Where are you?"

"I'm outside, Mom. Not near you." He was only a half an hour walk away, but he wasn't going to tell her that. He was already taking a major risk just simply by making the call itself.

"I...*found* something," she said. "After you left. I checked the pictures you were talking about. I sent the paramedics and police away. I'm scared, honey. I don't want to be here alone. Please come back so I can show you."

He looked at the sky. The moon and stars were at a brightness level that seemed to only occur on the coldest of nights. His toes hurt when he tried to wiggle them; his nose seemed to be perpetually running. He couldn't stay out here much longer.

"I'll come home, Mom. You promise me you're telling the truth?"

"Yes. Where are you? Let me come pick you up. You must be freezing!"

Dustin said, "I'm okay. I'm not far, and there's not a road near me, anyway. I'll be home in about half an hour. Is he there with you?" He meant Trevor.

"No," Desta said. "But I think I might know how to find him. God, you really saw him, Dustin? *Heard* him talk?"

"Yes. I'm going to start back right now. Keep the doors

locked. He might try to hit us at any time. We can figure out a way to stop him, put an end to this."

"Yeah, baby, we will. We have to." Desta sounded both heartbroken and terrified at the prospect of needing to confront her son.

"We do. I'll see you soon. Remember to keep the doors locked."

"I will. I love you so much, Dustin."

"I love you, too." So they *did* get to say it again to each other, after all.

Dustin hung up and slipped the phone in his pocket. He began the mile walk home. He took a break for five minutes at the halfway point, then continued onward. Somehow, some way, he believed tonight would be the end of everything, including possibly himself.

<------------->

He approached the house slowly. Every crackling of a leaf sent a bolt of electricity through his nerves, every sound of a car driving by causing his testicles to feel like they were being hoisted up into his stomach. He tip-toed to the left side of the house—no cop cars or ambulances on the street. He did the same on the right side—the curb was empty, nothing in the carport except for the Civic. He took out his phone and called Desta. She was at the back door and unlocking it ten seconds later.

"Dustin?" she called out softly. "Dustin, are you here?"

He stepped out from the trees. The light from the porch burned his eyes as he looked up at her. She was in her night-gown now, the lacy black one that she always wore a robe over. She was wearing one now.

"Can I come in?" Dustin said. "Like, I'm not gonna get tackled and catch a stun gun to the nuts, am I?" In spite of himself, he smirked a little bit.

Desta chortled. His vision adjusting to the light, Dustin could see how alarmingly pale she was. It looked like she'd aged ten years within an hour and a half. Whatever she'd found, it had been enough to scare her into a state he'd never seen her in before. She looked vulnerable, and that was not an easy feat to accomplish with Desta Taylor.

"You see anybody jumping out at you from the bushes? The SWAT Team went home for the night. Now, come inside. You're going to catch your death out here."

Or in there, his mind whispered.

"Okay."

She held the door open for him, and he went inside.

CHAPTER 21

O n the kitchen table sat the box of photos Dustin had gone through earlier. Displayed in front of it were various pieces of notebook paper, covered in scribbles of blue ink.

"I'm assuming you didn't look at the bottom of the box?" Desta asked.

"No," Dustin said while rubbing his chapped hands together, trying to get warm. Walking into the house was like living in an igloo and then coming out to discover you were actually in the middle of the tropics the entire time.

Desta sat down in the chair closest to the papers and picked up a sheet. She held it out to him by the corner, as if just merely touching it was like coming into contact with something tainted with anthrax. Dustin took it. Up close, he could see the paper was smudged with crayon markings, chocolate fingerprints, and dirt. Fresh dirt.

"He wrote those in the placements he went to after what happened with Craig," Desta said. "He was already getting drugs from that...*man* who died with him in the explosion. John. Read it."

Dustin took the paper and sat down in the chair across

from her. His extremities were beginning to feel like they were finally warming up. Now, he felt a chill run through him as he looked at Trevor's words, written in his own handwriting. The top center of the page read: *Trevor Taylor, February 4th, 2009.* Six months before he passed.

"He wrote this one while he was in the last placement he was sent to," Desta said. Dustin remembered well. Stonybrook Village, the one and only juvenile rehabilitation facility Trevor had escaped from. He'd lasted two weeks before simply walking away during outside work detail. Someone— probably John Brennegan—had picked him up and driven him back to Berthshire. Dustin and Desta didn't see him for one month after that, though plenty of other people in town had.

The note read:

I fuckin hate it here. The gay counsler and his bitch assistent can eat a fat hairy dick. So can mom. It's her falt I'm here. She said she was there for me but didn't protect me. Everyone's mad I do drugs and am angry all the time? Let them live thru what I did and do different.

I feel like I can't breathe most of the time. Mom let that faggot move into our house six years ago and that's how it all started. I see him in my dreams and nightmares. For my birthday that year I was wrapped inside of a box and they never even opened it. I finally got out myself.

Now it's not just dreams. I've seen Craig in reel life to, after he died. Before I came here he would come to my room at night. I saw him try to go to Dustin's once. He never lets me see him. It's always just this shadow in the shadows. All I can see are his wide eyes. It's like they glow in the dark. He never blinks. Just sits in the chair and rocks while he stares at me.

That's why I take Dustin with me when I take Mom's car at night. I don't want him alone in the house at night when I'm not there. Craig might take him. Then I get all fucked up and have him get all fucked up because I'm fucked up. He deserves to also be fucked up because he took Mom's attention away from me and also because Craig never hurt him. It's bullshit.

I told her about it and she won't believe me. She even laughed at me when I told her. Then I started crying and she hugged me. I don't want that bitch touching me. If (the rest of the paragraph was marked out by a Sharpie).

We'll see how funny it is when he comes for her. It's her fault, what happened to him. Yeah he was a motherfucker that tried to stand in between us, and I was the one who actually did it, but why am I being punished for it? I was just a kid.

At least I'm safe in here. It's so far away from the house, and there's no way it can find me. Even if it walked, someone would see it. It would be all over the news, like a reel life zombie story. But it's not a zombie...it's something so much worse. It can think. It knows what it's doing to me. Just keep me in here for as long as possible. Away from it.

Dustin put the paper on the table.

"That part he wrote about this Craig guy. Trevor said you laughed at him when you told him."

Desta nodded. "Yes, but it's not true. Not that part. Your brother's mind was almost completely gone when he wrote that. That's why I didn't believe him when he told me what he'd seen in his room or outside, but I never laughed at him about it. There's more."

Desta handed the next one over to him. This one was dated February 12th, 2009. Dustin began reading.

He found me. I don't know how. This place is three hours from home and he still fuckin' found me. No. It. It found me.

It comes to my window in the middle of the night. It throws stones at the glass til I wake up. I don't have a celly, so I'm always alone. I wish they'd put someone in here with me. It doesn't do that when the light's on or someone's doing a bunk check. Only when I'm alone, like it's just sitting out there for hours, watching until no one's around.

I used to get taken to the woods a lot. (The name was scratched out) would climb up to my window and make me go on rides. We'd go down to the same river John initiated me and Mark in. I'd be in the woods for hours, and no one would hear me scream. Adults are supposed to be your protecters, but all they ever did was hurt me when I didn't do anything to them. So fuck yeah I'm pissed at the world. It can burn in fucking hell for all I'm concerned. Specially after what I've seen. The world is hell.

Sober, I see how fucked up it is that I'm basically doing the same thing to my little brother. Not the super fucked up shit that happened to me, but the same idea of scaring him and taking advantage of him to make myself feel better. My therapist told me I'm only repeeting behaviers I know. Then she had me tied down and shot up with Thorazine when I told her Craig's back. Just another bitch, just like Mom

Sometimes I lay with the blanket over my head while it throws stones till it starts getting light out. Last night I looked out and it was right under the window. It was just staring at me like it did at the house. I saw its arm under the light pointing to the woods here. It wanted to take me there to do what it wanted to do to me for revenge. Where no one would hear me scream and no one would find me. Just like when (the remainder of the paragraph was scratched out again).

I called John today and told him to come get me. I'm going to dip during work releese tomorrow morning when they have me weed wacking. That thing will still be here. It's a couple mile walk thru the woods. I'm gonna kife a shaving razor tonight and make a shank. It's risky as fuck but I need a hit of speed, and need it bad. That's the only time I'm not scared.

. . .

Dustin read over the final paragraph again before handing the note back to Desta. She took it and tilted her head at the rest of the papers on the table.

"You want to read the rest? It's just more of the same stuff."

"No," Dustin said, thinking of the areas on the notes that had been blotted out. The ink looked fresh. Trevor must have altered them during his recent visit for some reason. "I've seen enough. But why do you believe me now after this? Trevor was on a shitload of different things. Like you said, his brain was probably fried by then."

"Because I saw it, too," Desta said in a husky voice. "Back then. It was late one night, and I had to go to the bathroom. I went in the hallway, and I saw a black shape in front of Trevor's door. It wasn't moving, just standing there. I would have walked right into it if it wasn't for the night light."

Dustin peered at her, his eyes gaped open wide.

"What...I mean, how did it react? What did you do?"

"I..." Desta started. "I walked right past it to the bathroom. I thought I was dreaming, like maybe a night terror. I came out a minute later, and it was gone."

"Was that the last time you saw it?" Dustin's voice was dry and cracking. Now, the room was not just warm, but *roasting*. Damp patches of sweat were visible in the armpits of his shirt.

"Yes," Desta said. "Trevor told me about it right before the end, but I thought it was the drugs talking, like I just said. I never knew until I found these pages tonight while you were gone."

Instinctively, Dustin's eyes flew to the door. Both locks were disengaged. He jumped to his feet and glided over there, clicking both of them into place. He looked through the glass as he did. Standing on the sidewalk, just barely outside of the light, was a frail, dark figure. The only feature he could make out was the eyes—impossibly white, unblinking, and locked dead on him.

"Mom," he squeaked out as his vocal cords lost any remaining moisture they had in them. "M-m-m-mom. Mommy, it's here."

Desta got up and joined him at the window. She looked out at the sidewalk, wrapping her hand around his and squeezing.

"Do you see it?" Dustin whispered. "See him? Is that Craig?"

"I see," Desta whispered back. "No, that's not Craig. Craig was a lot bigger. I think you're right. Somehow, the same thing happened to Trevor. He came back. And it makes sense, with everything you found in his room. Maybe you're right, and Trevor wants revenge."

How did she sound so calm right now? They were looking at the reanimated body of a dead person, and Mom was delivering exposition like they were having afternoon tea on a sunny day. Also, something about her tone, and the way she was saying things…

"What do you think it wants?" Dustin said. It still hadn't moved.

"I don't know. Maybe I should call the police back. I don't know what else to do, honey." She pressed herself closer to him.

"Stay there," Dustin said. "I'll get your phone. Where is it?" His phone had died right after the final call he made when arriving at the house, probably due to exposure from being in the cold for so long.

"In the living room," she said. "On the end table."

"Okay. I'm going to go get it. Stay right here, and watch it. If it moves, you let me know, okay?"

"Okay," Desta said, leaning into him more. "Just be careful."

"I will."

Dustin let her hand go and walked backward, never taking his eyes off the door until he passed into the living room. Then, he turned and bolted to the end table beside the couch, snatching Desta's phone off the charger. He went back into the kitchen and rejoined her at the door. He looked out. The figure was gone.

"Where did it go? Why didn't you tell me?"

"It walked off towards the woods," she whispered. "I saw it when it came into the light, and I couldn't...just...I just...*Oh my God*!"

Desta turned and grabbed Dustin, convulsively shaking while holding him in a death grip. He put one arm around her back and held the phone out with the other, opening it and pressing the green icon at the bottom right-hand corner.

His thumb was hovering over the dialer when he looked at the top of the screen. It was all of her recent calls. The first number on the top caused him to give pause.

Work, 4:49 PM

He did a double-take, making sure he was seeing what he thought he was seeing. One time, Dustin had to call 911 after he saw an old woman collapse outside the drug store when he was walking through town. The listing of *Emergency* had been at the top of his recent calls for the better part of a month before it was finally bumped down out of view. He wasn't much of a talker on the phone, unless he had to call work, or, more recently, Stacy. The only other person he talked to was his mother.

"Mom?"

"Yes, baby. What's the matter?"

"Did you really call anyone today to come and get me? Did you really call 911, or have an ambulance here?"

"Of course I did, sweetheart." Her mouth was right next to his face now. Her heaving breaths were being directed right into his ear canal. "I was worried about you. I never, ever want anything bad to happen to you."

Dustin yelped as her hand slipped down from his back and shot down, cupping him between the legs. He looked at the locks on the door. While the one on the knob was horizontal, the top one was pointed up and down, indicating it had been turned between the time he went to the living room and back. He felt a breeze on his arm. The door was partially open.

He pushed himself back from her, tripping over his own feet. Desta was looking at him with half-lidded eyes, her chest rising up and down rapidly. She slid the robe off, dropping it to the floor to reveal her negligee.

"Come on," she said breathily. "Let's go to bed, honey. We can lock the door so it can't hurt us. I'll take a knife and protect you. You never have to worry about anyone hurting you while I'm around."

Dustin held his hand in front of him, continuing to back up. As he did, he ran into the garbage can, toppling it over. He looked down, seeing among the refuse a silver bracelet, its shine dulled by streaks of brownish red all around it. Stacy's mother had given this to her as an 18th birthday present the month prior. She'd worn it everywhere she went.

"What the fuck...what the *FUCK*!?" Dustin couldn't catch his breath; his chest felt like it was constricting in on itself. He started to fade. Instantly, he employed his old trick of shoving his fingernails into his palm. Small pitter-patters were heard as drops of blood began dripping on the linoleum. Now, he hit his back against the wall as Desta waltzed towards him seductively. He had nowhere to go.

"Don't you need me, honey? Don't you *want* me? Tell me you need me, Dustin. Honey, please." Cloudy black streaks stained her cheeks as her eyeliner began to run with her tears.

"It was you," he said as he heard plodding footsteps ascending the basement stairs. "The horse, the note on the picture, Stacy. You did it all. But why?"

The knob on the basement door was beginning to jingle.

"I couldn't leave him like that," Desta said, a lone teardrop falling to the crease between her lips. "He talked to me. At the funeral, right before your uncle pulled you away from him. 'Save me. Save me, Mommy. Please, save me.' He *needed* me, baby. Just like you do. You don't know how nice it is to feel needed…to feel desired."

The stopper in the door clicked. It began pushing open slowly.

"The funeral? You've been letting him stay here the *whole* time, for six years!? And letting him do what he did to me…to Stacy?"

"No, I waited as long as I could," she said. "Then, I went there and…no one saw me because no one came to visit him. My little boy, in the dark, all alone. But he was there, honey. He was there, and he was alive. I freed him."

The basement door opened the entire way. What Dustin saw made him cry out at the top of his lungs. He wasn't fading anymore. In fact, he was *very* in touch with reality now.

"Stacy! Oh God, Stacy, what did they do to you!?"

Stacy stood in the doorway. She was completely naked. Her nipples were pebbled into hard pink stones, her lips cracked and chapped to the point they were slightly bleeding in places. There were purple and red welts all over the front of her body, as if she had been beaten repeatedly with a rod of some sort. Paired with these markings were open-palmed hand prints along her torso and genital region. A thin tendril of dried blood ran from her vagina to the center of her inner thigh.

"She's no good for you, honey," Desta said. "Look at her. Is that really someone you want to be with?" She had stopped just a few feet shy of him beside the kitchen table. The lace holding up the top of her nightgown had slipped down on both sides, exposing her breasts. This time, she did not attempt to cover them up. "You could be with me. With *us*."

"That's right, little bro," a voice he was very familiar with said from the doorway behind him.

Dustin watched as what had once been Trevor Taylor shambled past him, continuing until it stopped beside their mother. Seeing it standing there in a fully lit room was somehow even more terrifying than catching a quick glimpse of it under headlights in the dark. The state of its decay was *defined* now, making the impossibility all the more real. Dustin could see the outline of its ribs pushing against what was left of its dermal tissue. Its discolored skin was flaking everywhere, like wood from a log that had been tossed into a fire and taken out right when the outer layer was thoroughly charred.

"I told you I don't look so hot, bro-bro. Your bitch over there didn't even wanna play-play-play with me-me-me. But Mom made her play." It let out one of its choking laughs.

"Everything," Dustin said, astonished. "All of it. You knew what happened last month. You let him do it. In the woods, you knew who you were yelling at, and you knew you'd let him back in. Stacy…that's how she got here, in your car. *You* did it. And Craig and the abuse. *You* were the one who hurt Trevor. There was no Craig."

"No," Desta said while stroking Trevor's cheek with her finger. "There was a man named Craig. But he made a very big mistake. He tried to take you both away from me when he saw how close me and Trevor were. I couldn't live without you, so I decided he couldn't live at all. Then he came back and terrorized my boy. We took care of him again, though. Nobody will ever find him."

Dustin looked away as Trevor flicked his black tongue out and ran it along the side of their mother's neck. She leaned into it, soft moans escaping her lips. Stacy stood there watching it all, body swaying, blank eyes absorbing everything that was happening in front of them.

"The Bad Thing…you murdered him. You and Trevor."

Suddenly, Dustin had a flashback. It was a long time ago. He'd been wearing his favorite Power Ranger pajamas. There was loud screaming coming from down the hall. A man's voice—someone he knew. It was coming from his mother's room.

He ran down the hallway. Now he heard crying mixed in with the screams. The crying was high-pitched and slightly raspy. Trevor.

He reached up with his tiny hand and opened the door. It was unlocked. It was always unlocked. That way, Trevor could come in there late at night if he couldn't sleep. Dustin was allowed to, as well, but he never did. He *heard* what they did in there through the wall sometimes. He didn't like those sounds.

There was a lone white sheet on the bed. It was wrapped around something big and heavy-looking. Dustin remembered thinking the patches of red all over it were roses. Then he saw the ropes on the four corners of the bed, and then the hands and feet tied to them, jutting out from underneath the sheet.

"Go back to bed, baby."

This was the only dialogue he remembered from that night. He turned around to see Mom. She was standing in the bathroom; her arms and bare chest covered with the same shade of red as the roses. Sitting on the floor beside her was Trevor. He was also without clothes; his skin stained in the same dark red all over. In his hand, he held a large kitchen knife—the same one Mom had used to cut the pumpkin pie on Thanksgiving three weeks ago.

"Stacy," Dustin said gently. Her eyes slowly moved from Desta and Trevor over to him. "Stacy, come here."

She just stared at him, unmoving. It was obvious she was in shock, along with being severely dehydrated and in need of medical attention for her wounds.

"She got a new man, bro," Trevor said. "Someone to treat

her good-good-good." He flicked his tongue against Desta's earlobe.

In a flash, Dustin understood it all: his mother's constant yearning for attention and affection after his father died, her transferring the personality trait down to Trevor through her abuse, and then Trevor to Dustin. She'd never wanted Trevor to get better so his quality of life would improve. She wanted him to stop rebelling against what she'd done to him so he would be dependent on her again. When that didn't work, she enabled him by allowing him to stay at the house, despite what he was doing to Dustin. Even after death, Desta couldn't bear to let Trevor go—not because she missed him, but because she missed the feeling he once provided.

Things between her and Dustin had been fine all these years because she was able to control him through the trauma inflicted by Trevor's death. When he started growing up, doing all the things Trevor never had the chance to do, she couldn't take it, so she allowed Trevor to terrorize him again so her delusional hold would remain intact. Desta had to be the sole focus of Dustin's life, by any means necessary.

"After all she did to you," Dustin said to Trevor, "why me? Why are you putting me through this when it was her that did it?"

Trevor wrapped his gnarled hand around Desta's hair and pulled her head back. She gasped in surprise at the sudden and forceful way it handled her.

"You think it's just you-you-you? This bitch is getting what's c-c-coming to her, too." He slid his hand inside his pocket.

"Trevor, honey, what do you me—"

He pulled his hand out lightning fast, shoving three inches of a six-inch-long butcher knife into her stomach. She tried to scream, instead eliciting a high-pitched squeaking sound as she placed her hand on her torso and fell onto the table. Her other hand slapped against the wood, desperately trying to find something to hold onto. Her fingers found purchase on the edge closest to Dustin. As she tried to hold herself up, Trevor lifted the knife above his head and plunged it sideways into her back, almost burying it to the hilt. Now, she did let go and fell to the floor. Her blood eeled through the cracks of the tiles, mixing with Dustin's from when he'd dug into his palm earlier.

"Mom," Dustin said as an agonized expression stretched her features, morphing her face into something almost unrecognizable. He thought of all the times they'd joked around; when she would read him bedtime stories as a little boy; the birthday parties where she made sure to get party favors for all his classmates; when she would let him stay up late and watch David Letterman with her; her white-knuckling the dashboard as he practiced parallel parking on Orchard Street. All gone, mattering for nothing. He couldn't even cherish the memories after her death, knowing the self-centered, morally perverse reasons she had done it all for. All in one second, he grieved for two things: the woman he had thought she was, and the life of lies and manipulation that he'd never get back.

Forcing himself, Dustin looked at Desta's body and the deformed thing squatting over it. As he did, Trevor slowly turned its head until its infinitely insane gaze fell on him. Its lips were twitching and trying to move. It could have just been the result of shot and decaying nerve endings, but Dustin could have sworn that it was trying to smile.

"All done," it said. "Now, you-you-you. Only one man of the house. Sorry, bro-bro."

Dustin dashed towards the basement opening as Trevor sprung at him from its haunches. He'd moved just in time, causing the thing to hit the wall with a loud splat. Dustin moved into the opening and grabbed Stacy around the waist, pulling her back.

Trevor looked at him, head tilted as if it couldn't comprehend what just happened. Dustin held onto Stacy with one arm as he pushed the door shut with the other. The last thing he saw before it closed was Travor, standing up and walking towards him. Its shorts had fallen off during its collision with the wall. A set of deformed genitalia swung back and forth like a pendulum, its mutilated purple phallus pointed outwards in a hard straight line.

"You're quick, bro-bro," it said through the barrier between them. "All grown-grown-grown up-up-up!"

It smashed a hand against the door, causing it to instantly splinter down the center.

"You're a strong guy now!"

It hit the door again. This time, a small piece flew out, nicking Dustin on the arm.

Still supporting her, Dustin guided Stacy down the steps as the whole house seemed to be exploding from the sounds of the undead thing's rampage. They made it to the bottom after what seemed like forever due to Stacy's slow-moving state. Dustin looked around quickly, trying to find something in the room to defend them with.

Beside the washer/dryer combo was a kitchen chair—an old one that had gone with the table in the storage room. Dustin felt his heart ache as he saw a wooden pole covered in blood stains sitting on the floor beside it. There was an undeniable stench of bodily waste hanging in the air. He found the cause on the other side of the washer, spotting a bucket that was about a quarter ways filled with excrement. Stacy's makeshift bathroom while they'd kept her down here.

There wasn't time to hurt or feel sympathy now, only time to fight. Dustin looked up the stairs, seeing a large hole in the door. Trevor's arm was shoulder deep in it, hand wildly trying to find purchase on the knob.

Dustin dove to the floor, kicking up a cloud of dust. He grabbed hold of the bloody rod in a death grip and stood up, wielding it in front of him. Just as he did, the door exploded open in a shower of splinters and white paint chips. Trevor hobbled through the opening and began its way down.

"Trevor! Mark! Where's my shit, boys!?" Its accent took on a slightly southern quality. Its voice was no longer cracked and croaking, now back to the squalling demonic pitch it had used while screaming Dustin's name in the woods.

"Mr. Mommy Man, you better have my bitch ready, or I swear to fuck!" Chunks of mucus-filled dirt spilled out from its mouth to the stairs as it moved downwards. *"It's about to be a bad day for both of you motherfucker-fucker-fuckers!"*

Dustin carefully moved Stacy behind the washer and then walked out, holding the pole in front of him. Trevor was near the bottom of the stairs now. There was something...something down here that he was forgetting. Mom's ex, this Craig. He had come back the same way as Trevor. They had gotten rid of it somehow; Mom had said so. But how?

It comes to my window in the middle of the night.

That thing will still be here. It never sleeps.

We took care of him again, though. Nobody will ever find him.

Dustin looked to the Maytag. Something about it, something really important.

Trevor was at the bottom of the stairs now, just an arm's length away. Dustin held his ground, blocking Stacy, completely willing to die for her. He only prayed that if it killed him first, her ending would be quick and painless. After what Desta had allowed it to do to her, Dustin very much doubted that would be the case. He just had to think, remember. Craig, resurrection, Trevor, Maytag, basement...

"Hey, bro-bro," Trever said as it faced him. "What you gonna do with that—he nodded at the pole—beat me till I'm dead? A little-little-little brittle as a Skittle late for that. You could never beat-beat-beat me. You're Mommy's second little pussy, right next to that cock sucker we put down here. He just didn't have *the stuff!"*

It batted an arm at Dustin. He swung the pole at it like a

baseball bat. The dead thing let out a hiss as it connected with its forearm. It did this not because Dustin had hurt it, but because it was genuinely impressed at his speed.

Right next to that cock sucker we put down here. Was it talking about Craig? Down here, down here…Maytag…something there before…

"Good swing, little bro! Mom's t-ball lessons are really-really-really paying off!" The arm that had swung at him was hanging at an unnatural angle. If the Trevor thing felt the break, it gave no indication of it.

"Craig," Dustin said as the two stood at an impasse. "He came to you, he fucked with you in the same way you fucked with me. But he was right, though, wasn't he? Mom was doing stuff to you, and you needed to be taken away. But you didn't want that, did you, Trev?"

"Shut up." This was the first time the thing actually sounded like Trevor and not some cheap Creature Feature knock-off.

"You *liked* it," Dustin said. "You never said any of that stuff to me about Mom because you thought she was making me weak—you were *jealous*. Like your own mother was your ex-girlfriend or something. How fuckin' weird is that? No wonder you did drugs. You were already fucked in the head."

Dustin took a few steps back, but not out of fear, though he was feeling plenty of that right now. He remembered what was so important about Craig and the new washing machine. He just had to pray that what he was thinking would actually work. Even with a broken arm, that thing was never going to let them leave alive if it didn't.

"You don't f-f-fucking know-know-know, bro-bro, what I'm gonna do to you. I learned things over there. I can cut your head off and keep it alive long enough to watch your body die. Wanna see?" It swiped its other arm out, though not far enough to come into contact with Dustin. Having both arms out of commission would do it no good. It was slowly following him as he moved backward.

"*You* were Mommy's little bitch boy," said Dustin, his voice rising in pitch, taking on a mocking tone. "'Mommy took me into the woods and did bad stuff to me!' You were fucking *simping* over your own mom! Did you tell Mark and John about that? How your blood mother had touched you when you were little, and then how later you willingly climbed in bed with her, and you fucked—"

Trevor *lunged* at him like a feral animal. This time, Dustin wasn't fast enough. It knocked him to the floor and straddled him as its hands wrapped themselves around his throat. Dustin tried to look as far as his peripherals would allow him to. They were smack in the center of where he wanted them to be. The relief surging through him quickly washed away as he felt his windpipe being slowly crushed in on itself.

"Test me, fucking pussy? You wanna test *me*?" Now it *was* smiling, looking right down at Dustin as his cheeks went from beet red to a deep purple. "*Fuck-fuck-fuck with-with-with-with me-me-me!? I'll bring you back to life just so I can murk you again, bitch!*"

Dustin's hand desperately searched around the floor for the pole but could not find it—it had gone flying whenever Trevor tackled him. He tried to grab its arms and shift its weight so he could roll on top of it, but it had its knees firmly planted into the ground. It wasn't moving anywhere.

Dustin's vision was slowly narrowing into a dark tunnel, with Trevor's revolting face as the center. His limbs were growing numb.

"Do you *see* him?" Trevor asked, sounding genuinely excited. "The-the-the Void, bro. Look to the Void."

There was a slight shifting in the ground beneath Dustin's back. The square of dirt where the old dryer had sat. He barely registered it. Now, Trevor's face was being juxtaposed with something else over it. He would have called it another face, simply because there was no other word to describe it. Whatever it was, was huge, spanning at least the entire length of three galaxies. It had no discernible eyes, yet saw everything; no ears to hear, and yet knew every phrase a tongue had ever uttered, human or otherwise. It had no body except the darkness of the space around it, no physical boundaries because it existed in multiple planes at the same time. This wasn't the Ultimate, but the Ending before the Ultimate, the Demise before the Creation. This was what had control over the universe, and it was not pure.

The blackness within the blackness grew somehow even larger as Dustin began to float towards it. With each breath he was denied, the Void seemed to grow stronger somehow—joyous, even. He felt it every time his terror increased, like the area around him was emitting a higher level of electricity every time he wanted to scream.

Jesus, please don't let it speak to me, he thought incoherently. *I can deal with floating like this forever, but please don't let it speak to me. Christ, Father God. Please, no.*

To this, his prayer was answered. Besides a steady low-pitched hum, there was no sound at all. Just floating…floating…floating away into the Void…into Satan's maw.

"GET THE FUCK OFF OF ME! STOP! STOOOOOOOP!"

He was falling away now, not drifting anymore, but being jettisoned. The fibers of his cosmic being couldn't keep up with his consciousness. He was being ripped apart and reconstituted back together again at the same time. The Void was light-years away now, just a tiny dark blip in an ocean of greens, blues, and reds. Dropping, falling.

Dustin slammed back into his body with a painful thud. He greedily drank the air, his lungs feeling like they had a fifty-pound bag of sand in each one. The basement ceiling pulsated in his vision, every new pump of blood in his veins turning it a different color and size. His hands instinctively flew to his throat and massaged it. He tried to swallow a mouthful of spit, only to cough it back up as a screaming pain burned through his esophageal muscles. Life had returned, and with it came all the pains of near-death.

At first, all senses were blunted, like what he was experiencing around him was coming from a movie playing two rooms away. As the seconds went by, touch, taste, smell, and sight came back to him in their full glory. Finally, sound registered, as well. He used all of his strength to flip over and look at the source of the screaming that had brought him back.

"-FUCK OFF ME! GET OFF, GET OFF, GET OFF-OFF-OFF-OFF-OFF-OFF!"

The Trevor-thing was just above his head, kicking its mutilated feet in a frenzy. It was lying belly-first on the dirt, flopping its upper half up and down like a beached fish. All the sinister mocking and homicidal glee was gone from its voice now. In fact, it sounded positively terrified.

Dustin groaned as he assumed the push-up stance and lifted himself enough to see over Trevor's back. Around his shoulders were two arms even more decayed than his. Dustin could see stringy cords of marrow and muscle stretch and contract as the owner of them pulled Trevor closer to it. Whatever this other one was was much stronger, able to handle the elder Taylor brother with ease as it fought with all of its last dying strength against it.

"That's enough, Trevor. It's time to go back where we belong." Despite possessing the same gritty timbre of Trevor's voice, this new one sounded somehow gentler; safe.

"FUCK *YOU!*" Trevor spat back. "I'm not going back-back-back-back-back, serious as a heart attack! I just need my glass, then I'll be right as rain! Someone get me my pipe-pipe-pipe! *SOMEONE! GET! ME! MY! PI—*"

The words were cut off as the other thing grabbed

Trevor's head on either side and ripped it clean off from its spinal column. The random chunks of dirt and stone flying through the air ceased. All was silent for a moment. Then, the arms reached up and grabbed Trevor's headless body, dragging it into the ground. The area inside the square seemed to come alive as it went from hard earth into muddy quicksand, swallowing Trevor's head, the thing that had once been Craig Jefferson, and what remained of Trevor's body. When no traces were left, the ground simply packed itself back up and ceased in its movement. Dustin reached a hand out, tentatively poking it with his pointer finger. Solid dirt.

He rolled over and lay there for a while, trying to catch his breath. As he finally felt his head begin to clear, he heard a light skidding noise somewhere above him. He tilted his head up, ready for the worst. What he saw brought a torrent of tears to his eyes and a smile to his face.

"Stacy," he barely managed to get out. "Stacy. Thank... thank God."

She was still naked, that far-off look present in her eyes. In her hands, she absently held the pole that had gone flying earlier. The top of it had something purple around it. Dustin looked closely, seeing the text stenciled across it *All Eyez on Me*. A piece of Trevor's shirt. It was wet with a dark reddish stain. The Trevor-thing had been able to bleed, after all.

"You-you-you...helped save me," Dustin said. "You're still there, somewhere."

To this, Stacy responded by continuing to stare off into space. Dustin slowly pulled himself to his feet and embraced her, uncaring of the intimacy such an action entailed.

"I'll never leave you," he whispered into her ear. "But I also won't ever hurt you. Never, never, never, never!"

He was still holding her and crying into her neck when there was a creaking from above, followed by the ear-shattering shriek of a woman.

Mom was still alive.

CHAPTER 22

Dustin and Stacy climbed the stairs and entered the kitchen. A wide snail trail of blood was smeared across the floor from the table to the opening in the hallway. Dustin left Stacy and followed it. Along the wood of the hall ran the same greasy stain. It made a sharp turn and stopped in front of one of the doors. The storage room.

Dustin followed it on the balls of his feet, careful not to make a noise. Arriving, he held a shaking hand out and turned the knob. The door squeaked on its hinges as he slowly pushed it open.

It was like he'd entered a time capsule. Trevor's room had been perfectly restored back to its original state. On the walls were the posters from the bin Dustin had searched earlier. A large, glossy picture of Mac Miller looked out at him from right above Trevor's old bed, put back together with the blanket tucked so perfectly into the frame that a pin would bounce if dropped on it. One of the old end tables was sitting beside the wall. On it were various glass pipes and lighters, along with a syringe, half-filled with brown liquid. Two blue rubber tourniquets sat beside the paraphernalia. This was why Desta had scared him out of the house with the fake 911 call earlier; she'd wanted to set up Trevor's room for after the family reunion was done.

He heard a deep wheezing coming from behind him and turned slowly, already knowing what he was about to see.

Desta sat with her bleeding back against a wall of storage totes. In her mouth was a half-smoked Marlboro menthol. Her cheeks were devoid of color, and one eyelid seemed to have lost the ability to open on its own. In this state, she finally looked like how she felt on the inside: helpless, old, alone. Her working eye rolled in its socket until it finally found Dustin.

"Hey, baby," she said, letting out a strangled cough. Small speckles of blood landed on her nightgown top and chest. "Could you…get the sweet peas from the cabinet for me? I put them…in…the top shelf…this time." She blew out a lungful of smoke without taking the cigarette out of her mouth. Dustin bent down and plucked it away, allowing her to breathe clean air.

"Mark that in your mind," he said, dropping the butt on the floor and stomping it out. "If you live through this, that's going to be the last thing I ever do for you. I hope you die alone, paralyzed, and without a soul in the world to feel sorry for you. And they won't. Not after they hear my story."

With that, he turned his back on her and began walking away. He heard a loud thump behind him, followed by the sound of Desta dragging herself along the carpet. He did not turn to look.

"Dustin…baby, *please*! You don't know how much I love you! Please, baby, *please*! It hurts so bad. I might die here. Honey, sweetie, baby! I don't want to die here alone! Please, *DON'T LET ME DIE HERE ALO—*"

Her voice was cut off as he closed the door behind him. He joined Stacy in the kitchen and dialed 911. By the time he had her dressed and the paramedics arrived, he was in the corner of the living room beside the couch, crying hysterically.

The Void looked down upon him and smiled.

ALSO AVAILABLE FROM NIGHTMARE PRESS

THE GUARDIANS
Teresa Sewell & Rob Le

In a mystical world where lycans and vampires rule, where magic, cruelty, and blood are part of everyday
life, in a time if good fails then all is lost, fate rests in the hands of three people. Three spoken of in a
forgotten legend from a race destroyed long ago—or a perhaps a race long hidden from those who seek to
destroy them.

Brenat and Teera believe they'll never conceive. However, a miracle happens during their bonding on the
night of the blood moon, bringing the couple both surprise and joy. When a second miracle occurs, and
they find themselves with seven children, they dream of raising their family in the safety of a small,
hidden valley.

Threatening their dream are those who want the children for their own evil schemes. The eldritch witch
Keres and her wicked master seek to annihilate all that is good in the world. Believing the family to be

those spoken of in the ancient legend of creation, Keres and her master set out to gain control of the

children and convert them to evil so they can rule the world.

However, they are not the only ones with nefarious plans for Joel and his siblings...

ACKNOWLEDGMENTS

There were a lot of different factors that went into writing this book. Is it the best thing I've ever written or will ever write? I'm not sure. As I type this section right now, I'm still very numb coming out of the past eight years, a time filled with a lot of self-inflicted emotional pain, addiction, and chaos. Originally, I just wanted to create a simple horror novel, one that would help me get outside of my own head and focus on something not related to the struggles I was personally experiencing. That turned out not to be the case, as the entire piece is wrought with themes of codependency, fear of abandonment, manipulation, gaslighting, lying, and a plethora of other issues that I myself was working through, both from an internal and external standpoint.

So, back to the question of where this work stands within my catalog of other novels, I can't say if it's the best thing I've ever done, but it is the most important one. It helped me to face a lot of my demons and regain the will to write creatively during my darkest times, and so, for me, while it may not objectively be the "best" from the world's point of view, it is to me.

I want to give a HUGE shout-out to Oil Region Recovery in Polk, PA, for being the other half of the beginning of my alcoholism recovery journey. It took five tries in 2025, but I think I finally got it, with the help of the wonderful staff and numerous clients that I encountered there. I was on the brink of death at least three times within eight months, not to mention the numerous other brief stays I had there before that, and they patiently and lovingly welcomed me back each time, instilling information and lessons into my soul that I will carry with me for the rest of my life. Through the grace of Christ, they saved my life, and I shall remain forever grateful.

To Joe, Analiza, Nick, Cooper, and everyone else from the church that I was involved with, thank you for taking me in and providing me the environment to get a couple of months of sobriety in me. I did a lot of shady things to get here, and you all forgave and helped me when you had no earthly reason to.

The same goes for my dear friend, Eric, who took me in after I could no longer function or be around the previous people who helped me. You accepted me when I had nowhere to go, and you were still willing to take me in after I fell and broke your trust. There is a special place in Heaven waiting for you, my friend.

I will throw a thank you in to Abby. I was an anxious mess, multiple times, and you had the patience and a caring heart to sit with me and help me work through it. That is not an easy thing for someone to do, especially with the likes of me.

Special thanks to Amy and Devin, along with Shaylin, Chrissy, Sherri, Corey, Brenda, and anyone else who was there and tolerated me through that period. I probably wouldn't be here if it weren't for you all, and thus, this book would have never been written, which I egotistically think would be a real shame, though others may disagree. I had been alone, killing myself every night without a soul in the world to know about it. Exposing that to you guys is what kickstarted the revelation that I actually needed to take this seriously before I hurt myself or worse. You all allowed this work to be a possibility, but more importantly than that, you saved a life, and that deed can never be repaid.

For Tyler and Collin, who basically saw me die right in front of them and still stood with me after that. I apologize to you guys for putting you through that, as well as Leah. Again, as a running theme, I would not be alive without you fine fellows.

A warm mention to my friend, Alex, who had to make the difficult decision to back away while I was in the midst of addiction. You were a giant support during that time. Without your kind words, I would not have sought assistance or had my first two months sober in order to be where I am right now. Your words of kindness and wisdom inspired me to do that, and also gave me the insight to look internally and see that I was the problem, not everyone around me. This was the revelation that saved my life, and you were a big part of that.

Dave from Necro Publications. You are no longer here with us now, but you gave me my start in this game when you really didn't need to. Without you, I would not know even the first thing about how to properly write a novel or all of the technical finesse that goes into it. Our conversations were tense and even blatantly contentious at times, but you still believed in my ability and kept giving me chances when no one else would. Also, you gave me the advice to "start off your story with something big, so it grabs the reader's attention." Instead of making the story of Trevor Taylor some kind of supernatural mystery, this philosophy allowed me to get that right out of the way and dive into the heart of the story. I try to follow this advice with everything I write.

Katrina, who has always been a wonderful friend to me even when I haven't been to her. Keep the sun shining in New Zealand, and please, please take the Vote for Trump sign out of your yard. Your neighbors are talking about you, whether you know it or not.

I can't forget my girl, Jamie, who has made some awesome crafts for me and sent them from California. It's always a bright spot when I have the opportunity to talk to you, and it's also something that has kept me going, even in my of worst times.

To the unnamed friends whom I do not speak to anymore: without our relationships, I wouldn't have realized that holding onto the past is what was dictating my future, hence why many of you had to step away. I fully understand why you did it, and I thank you so much for providing me the kind of tough love I needed in order to find the will to live again.

And a special thanks to Jacob Floyd, who trusted me enough to accept this book without even knowing what it was about or before I had anything from the handwritten version typed yet. I will always be your First Lady at Nightmare Press, and don't you ever forget that, honey buns.

For anyone else I may have forgotten to mention, just know I love and value every one of you and your contributions into my life. A novel is a fictional representation of our combined experiences and knowledge, gained from those we encounter in day-to-day life. Without you, there is no me, and thus no writing. You're just as much a part of this process as I am.

To all the addicts and abused people still suffering out there: hold on, take it day by day, and keep moving. There is a light at the end of the proverbial tunnel. Sometimes, all it takes is for someone to open our eyes so we can see it.

ABOUT JOHN

John "Bobby" Shupeck is a mean cat from the darkest depths of the Pittsburgh streets. His hobbies include knifing skeezers, shooting dice in a trap house, and sleeping under a bridge. He has also written ten other published works, mostly about his love of the game and how to properly "Crip Walk." Any donations would be both encouraged and appreciated.